AVADHOOT DONGARE started writing fiction in 2007. He has published four novels in Marathi: *Svatahala Faltu Samjanyachi Goshta* (The Story of Being Useless, 2012), *Eka Lekhakache Teen Sandarbha* (Three Contexts of a Writer, 2013), *Paan, Pani Ni Pravah* (Leaf, Water and Flow, 2015), and *Bhintivarcha Chashma* (Specs on the Wall, 2018). The first novel was awarded the Sahitya Akademi Yuva Puraskar in 2014. He has also published a critical essay *Svatahacha Avakash Tapasatana* (Probing One's Space, 2017) about one of the translations he had done as a professional and a book of short stories for children. He blogs at ekregh.blogspot.in.

NADEEM KHAN has been a teacher of English since 1973. For more than seven years he worked as Director, Western Regional Centre, Amravati, of the Indian Institute of Mass Communication, an autonomous institute of the Ministry of Information and Broadcasting, Government of India.

He has translated into English the writings of well-known Marathi novelists Bhau Padhye and Vishwas Patil, Hindi short-story writer Doodnath Singh, as well as artists Ram Kumar and Jangadh Singh. He has also translated Sathya Saran's *My Daughter – My Shakti* from English to Hindi.

He is a voracious reader and his lectures on a variety of subjects have been very popular in academic and corporate circles for over twenty years.

News! How much newness does any news have? What news-value do the non-new things carry? There are things, incidents and people that do not make news. They do not possess enough newness for the news-hungry world. These things and beings are useless for the manufacturers of news.

Among these manufacturers is a young sub-editor interning with a Marathi newspaper who looks at things that are mundane – no use for the news. Does he discover something in the mundane? Does he find anything more meaningful there than just making up news? This is The Story of Being Useless.

A writer writes or types. Where does his writing start and where does it end – and what is in between? What does he want to say and what does he want to hide? What lies beneath this façade of letters and words and sentences? What holds together the structure within? Why is this structure created in the first place? What about the writer who has written this novel or novella? Has he really created something novel or is it just a re-rendering of the old?

This is a story of a typist, well, a writer, who wrote 'The Story of Being Useless' and who is writing Three Contexts of a Writer.

RATNA TRANSLATION SERIES

The Story of Being Useless
&
Three Contexts of a Writer

— TWO NOVELLAS —

AVADHOOT DONGARE

TRANSLATED FROM MARATHI BY

NADEEM KHAN

RATNA BOOKS

Published by RATNA BOOKS
An imprint of Ratna Sagar P. Ltd.
Virat Bhavan, Mukherjee Nagar Commercial Complex
Delhi 110009, India
www.ratnabooks.in

Contents

The Story of Being Useless

To
Jack Kerouac

One

Can't quite say exactly when I began to know him. Can't give the exact date, but roughly, yes. A tree came crashing down in the Department of Journalism on 20 January 2009. That was when Barak Obama was sworn in. Or a little more than a year ago, tiny Kosovo had buggered Yugoslavia and jumped out. Or the Darfur mess was on in Sudan. Or Mumbai November 2008. Or Abhinav Bindra got his gold medal in the Beijing Olympics. Or A.R. Rahman got his Oscar. Or Sachin Tendulkar hit 200. Or on 13 March 2010 Kanu Sanyal committed suicide.

Exactly when he started considering himself as useless, can't quite say. Basically, so many things were happening, people were talking so much – who wants to sit in all that muck searching for the exact time he started considering himself useless? But it was around sometime then he was walking down Lakdi Pul. When he reached Alka Talkies he saw children of varied shapes, some clothed, some naked, stretched out, entangled on the road. The situation was such that there was no space left for getting past them. Grill and road on the left, grill and river down there on the right. He then noticed a smallish figure, and planting his right foot on the earth he hopped over it, left foot forward. Just then, a straw-haired woman in a yellow blouse and a green sari pounced upon him. She was enraged by his leaping over the child. But he could really have done nothing. If she had really landed him one on the neck, he couldn't have done anything at all.

However, moving along the edge of Tilak Road, he managed to reach his room in the cramped flat in an old run-down building at Sadashiv Peth. There were three rooms in that flat. Open the latch and you get into a dark, narrow passage. This room on the left. The right one is Uday's. The next one on the right belongs to the two Bengalis. Opposite that is the attached bathroom.

There's a table in the room, a small steel almirah. There's a tattered mattress, and there are bugs in the mattress. There's a window, wooden frame painted white. One of the grime-laden panes is gone, a cardboard piece fixed in its place. Came with the room. A rusted fan. And the usual mess.

By the time he switched on the fan and stretched out on the cot, he was soaked in sweat. He didn't know what he would have done if the woman had really let one fly. He couldn't have done anything anyway. A rickshaw-man had once held him by the collar. The guy had wanted the 28 rupee fare rounded to 30.

He said, 'How's that? 28 means 28.'

He said this twice, and the rickshaw-guy just kept looking

at him. Then said, 'Get the change.'

Now he didn't have 28 bucks in change, so he said he'd get it from the grocer's.

The rickshaw-guy, on the edge already, said, 'Go fuck your mother.'

Going direct to mother? So he too got back, 'Go fuck your mother, bhadvya. Who you abusing?'

As he said this the rickshaw-guy stepped out and held him by the collar, saying, 'Know who I am?' He thought he could stand up to the rickshaw-guy; the fellow wasn't much in build, see? Heavy voice though. Then people gathered. He went for the rickshaw-man's collar but somebody pulled him back. Two-three people were pulling the rickshaw-guy away too, telling him to let go.

'Maadarchod, know where Morey Colony is?' said the rickshaw-man.

He: 'Your mother's beat?'

Both were now a few inches from each other. Then people sat the guy in his rickshaw. A few more abuses – from the rickshaw-man to him, from him to the rickshaw-man. Lasted barely a minute, this scuffle. The rickshaw fellow lost his 28 bucks, pointlessly. Nobody banged nobody.

For a minute he was brimming with confidence. 'Let's see what happens, chyaayla!' This and whatever else. But nothing really happened. Then he suddenly crashed. Crashed means down flat. Should run away somewhere, somewhere far away. It had happened at Sinhgad Road. Should get to Pune University, he thought. Somewhere deep inside. There's a bank there, so behind that. Or inside the Department library somewhere, he felt. It didn't happen thus though.

❖

A state-level newspaper, basically from Mumbai, but its Pune edition. May of 2009 was coming to a close when he started going there as a trainee reporter. The paper held intellectual sway. The weekend supplements were weighty. But the Pune edition had turned drowsy. Four-five trainee kids – some doing the course – some looking for jobs post the course – some tiring looking for jobs – and three or four absolutely star reporters – chipping in with their reporting bits and pieces – an occasional bit from this or that young subber. Occasionally, a guy from the editorial department would leave. The others would have to pull the slack. Pages however would continue being made. Brought out. He had done his internship there during the course. So he had an idea of the circumstances there. So it's not as if he started considering himself useless after he started working there. It had begun earlier. No way of finding out exactly when. But certainly before the tree fell in the department.

The people who were there when the tree fell aren't there any more. How many keep coming and going, who knows? But the Journalism Department building has been right there for a hundred years. A stumpy stone and shingle structure with 'The Ranade Industrial and Economic Institute, Poona 1910' stamped on its square forehead. But that's just the name. Inside are the Department of Communication and Journalism and the Department of Foreign Languages of Pune University. These two departments, broken off the main acreage of the Pune University at Chaturshringi, sit silently on this campus at FC Road. As you enter the gate, there is a two-wheeler parking to the right. A tree there came crashing down on 20 January 2009. A tree fell and a shade disappeared. There were other shades on the campus, true. The ramshackle tin and wood canteen behind the building, under the gulmohar tree, its dark shade spreads out too. But the shade of that tree disappeared, equally true. But there were all those myriad shades still there, also true. Shades – shadows – shades. The thin shade when the slanty sunshine strikes the rough stones of the wall, the shadow of the shingles that hits the top part of the wall, the big and small shadows of the stones scattered across the ground, the shades of the wooden doors, the shades of the windows, the shadows of the tiny little stones of the steps that stood in bunches of two and three. The shades of the trees that were still around. Oh, plenty.

There were plenty of things happening. Causing turmoil everywhere. Some of them were published in the papers. In the middle of this confusion he sat in the library, reading a newspaper. Dense clouds out there. It was three in the afternoon, but the darkness was such that another would have switched on the tubelight. He, however, sat in the dark reading the paper. Lots of papers spread across the cuddapah slab in front, and inside the library – dark.

The library is set in a small patch in the rear part of the stone building. Fifteen stubby, ancient wooden cupboards with square-paned shutters – three slightly bigger steel almirahs – a narrow passage through the cupboards – stone steps to the right – a small room on the left – a slightly bigger table inside there, four-five chairs – a locked wooden door in a corner – a long narrow passage to the right of the stone steps

– big wooden windows with smoky panes in the left wall – a long cuddapah slab in the same wall for use as a table – seven-eight chairs scattered from here to there – eight-seven papers littered from there to here – two fans on top, one working, the other not – above the fan and in every corner: plenty of cobwebs.

It was August of 2008. And he in the dark department library. Outside, the rains were on the verge of descending. The soft shadows of the trees on the cuddapah slabs. *Loksatta – Sakaal – Indian Express – Prabhaat – Navaa Kaal – Times of India – Navbharat Times – Kesari – Maharashtra Times – DNA – Free Press Journal – Asian Age – Hindu* – the papers of that date lay in a merry mess. They generally get whisked up by 3 o'clock. A tall heap of old newspapers in a corner of the slab.

There was a small write-up in an inner page of the Free Press Journal saying something about how tea quaffing increases life-span. But he couldn't get into it because Ramchandra Parab burst into the library with a loud 'Heyyyyy'. Then laughed. Ramchandra switched on the tubelight. The white light washed across the library and the pale shadows vanished. Ramchandra entered and pushed the papers to one side.

'These guys have fucked journalism, pal,' he said, and sat on the cuddapah.

Ramchandra has lately started saying this quite a lot. The earlier Ramchandra was quite different. His enthusiasm in the first year was boundless. That was in the beginning. He would talk to a lot of people then. Talked a lot. This was Ramchandra till roughly the end of the first semester. Would try speaking in English. Expressed opinions on almost every issue. All this petered out later. After the internship, he came right down. In the second semester, right, right down. His visits to the department came down too. He had done his internship with a small paper. He had had some unpleasant experience there. The rest too was like it happens all the time. Next year onwards, he was regularly heard saying that journalism was fucked.

That day, Ramchandra took him straight to the canteen for a cup of tea. The one behind the building. Tin sheets balancing on steel pipes spread across the empty spaces under the gulmohar. Wooden planks for sitting. A few plastic chairs here and there. A low iron table. Another square one, slightly bigger. A wooden bench placed across. Earth direct under the feet. A barbed-wire-topped stone ledge nearby marking the end of the department campus. The cash counter at the wooden table resting under a semicircular roofing of cement sheets. Big black skillet on the side. A tin-sheet-reinforced wooden table next to it. The tea-vending Lala with bulging veins, and steam.

'What's going on between them these days?' said Ramchandra. Sayli Jadhav and Jayesh Shinde were sitting behind. Sayli Jadhav was in black jeans and a green top, and Jayesh Shinde clad in blue jeans and a checked light-blue half-sleeved shirt was telling her something. She was smiling a bit. There was nothing unusual in this either, just another subject for Ramchandra other than journalism.

'Saw them the other day at Shivajinagar.' When Ramchandra said this, he felt a little bad for Ramchandra. Looked at the two, and felt a little bad for himself.

It was overcast outside. Looked like it would rain. Lala was making tea. Right at the other end, beyond the bench visible behind Sayli Jadhav's mane, the three-legged dog was peacefully napping, as always. There was a biggish piece of paper lying next to him. Little gusts of wind would make Sayli Jadhav's hair blow and make the paper dance in tandem. There on the other side and here, too, leaves were floating in the air. Somebody said: 'That seems romantic.' Could well be one of those two who said it. Everything adrift – senselessly! Good too, despite what Ramchandra had to say. Meanwhile, the tubelight in the library was still aglow, needed switching off. Not many people were around that day at that time. Those two were talking, Ramchandra was talking. The wind calm. The dog was quiet. The paper flew. The hair flew too. The leaves swirled. The air was nippy.

Two

Nice that it was raining. Nice also that the papers were coming out. Whatever whoever might say, and however much, it was nice that the papers were coming out. Can't say that it was exceedingly good, but nice, certainly. Coming out in the world, coming out in India, coming out in Maharashtra. Arriving at the library, arriving at this and that village, arriving in the towns.

Journalists were aplenty too. Goggles-wearing, non-goggles-wearing. Jacket-clad, non-jacket-clad. There were those who considered the world chootiya, and those who didn't. Those who filched articles from the internet, those who just didn't write. Those who covered the district, those who made the district pages. Those doing cities, making city pages, translating the agency stories, hordes of them. Sitting astride the Journalists' Union, journalists who never wrote a piece of their own. Those who thought they knew the inside story of everything, those who stayed away from all this.

Over-enthusiastic journalists, over-unenthusiastic journalists. When the over-enthusiastic became still more enthusiastic and the over-unenthusiastic became still more so, he was doing the engagement diaries and the notices. The whir of the AC by his side.

There in the last passage sit the reporters. The passage so narrow it was a hassle going past the chairs with their backs to each other. He sat on the last chair. A heap of pressnotes on the table in front. Send poems for this one, send articles, something else for that one. Bride-bridegroom matching meets, conferences, lectures, anniversaries, all such clamour. Tomorrow's programme diary, open beside him, as he did the notices. The whir of the AC in the neighbourhood. The wired grimy window open. Out in front, water was dripping. In the building beyond, girls and boys coming for classes were playing around with each other's bodies. Pieces of cardboard lying under the AC here.

He was arranging the programmes time-wise in the engagement diary. The chief reporter walked in suddenly. Tall, big-built, half-sleeved shirt tucked in, bag slung on the right shoulder. Said, 'How's life treating you?' Put the bag down, removed his cap and started the computer. 'Want to work in the editorial department?' he asked.

He stayed quiet, so the chief reporter carried on, 'You'll get 5000 bucks in the bank account, and a straight employees' contract from the company like everybody else.' 'Will do,' he said. Trainee boys there got 1500, and that too through cheque, every four-five months, no official stamp of the newspaper either. This was much better. 'Apply for the sub-editor's post,' the chief reporter said.

The paper was going to sleep; things were being dragged along somehow by getting boys to work on low wages. The company owners didn't care for the editors, and the Mumbai editors didn't care for the resident editor at Pune. Under the circumstances he applied to the resident editor for the sub-editor's post and thanked the chief reporter. The man had at least done what was within his powers. Because of that he would at least be getting 3500 more, and on time too.

Reporter or sub-editor, for the outsider, it's just a journalist. Forget what importance who carries, people read the newspaper, and the names that show there show.

Don't know the name of the old waste-paper man.

The old man sits in the empty space on the edge of Lakdi Pul solving crossword puzzles in the *Navaa Kaal* with a chewed up pen. The beat of this collector of discarded cardboard is fixed. Kumthekar Road, Bajirao Road, a little bit this way and that, Appa Balwant Chowk.

At peak afternoon the old man arrives at the empty space on Lakdi Pul and sits there, solving puzzles. Full-sleeved, thick, bluish T-shirt, trousers short even for his short frame, beard grown right up to his throat, ruffled hair, thick wrinkles on the face, and deep penetrating eyes, the dust-laden old man sits solving puzzles. Well before the evening truly sets in, the old man moves off. He had a bicycle earlier. He would then hang the cardboard stuffed plastic bags to his cycle and set off. But then he sold it to the mustachioed man who runs his bicycle business around Lakdi Pul on the Karve Road side. The old man now carries the cardboard stacks directly in his hands or in plastic bags swinging from his hands.

Most of the time the old man piles his little stock behind Maharashtra Bank on Tilak Road. The old man is short. Tough. Rough. Right there on Tilak Road, he often has his afternoon tea at the Ambika Amrut-tulya – Pune term for tea stall. Buys the *Navaa Kaal* almost every day from a newspaper stall on Bajirao Road. Sits through the afternoon solving crossword puzzles with his chewed up pen. Never heard a single word breaking out of the old man's mouth. Not saying that he never spoke, or couldn't speak. With all those word puzzles lined up before him, what would he speak any way, chyaayla?

Asked the old man why he felt like spending money every day for reading a newspaper. The old man's misty eyes turned melancholic. If he buys a newspaper every day, it's obviously because he wants to. But asked him anyway. Didn't say a word, the old man. Asked him if he wanted another cup of tea. Old man doesn't speak. Asked, 'Want another pen?' Old man doesn't speak. Go mad asking, but old man doesn't speak.

His acquaintance with the old man stretched back three years. They have known each other since the monsoons of 2006, or thereabouts. What happened was that he was walking down Bajirao Road when the rain arrived as he hit the Kelkar Museum Lane. Seemed sharp enough to wet you, so he ducked towards the rusty tin sheet on the right. Narmadeshwar Amrut-tulya. It was proper rain, and when five minutes went past, he got into the cavern and ordered tea. Before the tea arrived, there was the dripping old man outside. Must be a regular here, got his tea without the asking. Shelled out three bucks on the spot. Not soaked through, but he was quite wet. But hung on outside. His left arm was getting a proper wetting, but no tension. He was in a completely soiled white shirt and loose pajamas. His health then, to tell the truth, was better.

This event too was a long time ago. Since then, the old man has been sighted on almost a permanent basis.

The old man outside the Journalism Department, and inside – the three-legged melancholic dog. No tension. The dog, of course, began as a four-legged creature. But some time ago, meaning a few years ago or thereabouts, some kind of accident occurred or something, and his right fore leg got smashed. The chap got to limping around with his smashed leg. Even otherwise he rarely drifted outside the department campus; even that stopped for good after the leg got smashed. Later, a Delhi girl who took a fancy to him took him to a doctor and got his leg cleaned up. Now that brown spotted white dog moves around properly on his three good legs. The department campus now takes care of his upkeep. So no tension about his livelihood.

When the tree fell, the dog was sitting in a library corner staring wistfully at nothing.

Beyond the department walls, there is no relationship between this dog and journalism. The overall situation is that there is no relationship between the dog and anything else, really. The dog is exactly as much at peace as the department campus.

Three

Looked at one way, there was commotion; looked at another, stillness all around. Plenty of people in the office, really. Twenty odd people in the editorial department. Ten odd in reporting. Matter trifling, but proofreaders seven or eight. Operators seven. Scanning guys three. Peons three. This number can generate plenty of noise, but they don't, actually. The resident editor spoke very loudly. A peon bellowed. A proofreader laughed out loud. There were other noises, besides.

With this backdrop, Karle was whispering into his ear that all this would move to Mumbai. There was nothing new in what Karle said. He knew it too, Karle knew too that he knew it, everybody knew it. The entire editorial department would move to Mumbai, with just a bureau here, the game plan being that the local edition would be brought out only as a front for advertisements. The delay was on account of some people whose chairs were important. Meanwhile, the fun game was on.

Lots of fun.

For instance, tall young bald Malusare tells short semi-bald Sarmalkar, 'Hey, Sarmalkar, should we have a sitting today?'

'But I am sitting, ain't I?' – Sarmalkar.

'Not this. How about sitting with us this evening?'

'I sit here all through the day. So why again in the evening?'

'Gosh, Sarmalkar, don't you occasionally tipple a bit?'

'When I feel tippled without actually tippling, why go for tippling?' This is a typical Sarmalkar-style statement.

It was enough to make Malusare laugh. Sarmalkar laughed too. Fun.

Whatever, however much, fun it was. Not as if it was all fun, but some of the stuff was funny.

Even now, in that paper, the sub-editors made the pages themselves. Meaning, no hassle of getting the pages made from the artists.

The pages were of eight columns. News had to be filled in there. News of single column, double column, triple column. Photos, captions, point, font, page making. The advertising guys would fit the advertisements in the requisite spaces. The remaining space to be filled with news – sub-editor's job.

Karle was one among the many unenthusiastic sub-editors. The determination with which he stayed unenthusiastic was amazing. The work is not less, but not more either. Stayed out of this, and stayed out of that. Karle had been right there for fourteen long years. Karle had been sub-editor for enough years to blow one's mind. Yet, Karle was different. He never ran a person down indiscriminately, nor praised someone indiscriminately. Now, look, all this can't be proved, really. And while having tea, he would occasionally shoot off in all directions, but only occasionally. On the whole, he just refused to give opinions; hence, there was no issue of good and bad. Opinion, if given, would be general, and never about a person. From the day he joined work about a year back, Karle has been like that. Can't say how he was before that. Karle would come. Translate the PTI news. Make the pages. Have tea. No talking. Karle was gloomy, but he was fun. He was not a great journalist, meaning he was not famous. But he had no interest at all in talking about the famous. He had no interest in talking about the non-famous. Impossible to say what Karle was interested in. Loose half shirt, dark trousers, hair more white than black, thin moustache, spectacles, a touch shorter than normal. Karle just was. Karle taught him to make pages.

'We are big-time sex-maniacs,' – Mahesh Kadam's dirty talk made him feel good. Abuses help the head stay balanced. Mahesh Kadam needs no reason to turn abusive. Mahesh got married last month. When he came back after a month's leave, he said, 'We are sex-maniacs.'

'After doing it all you say this?' He.

'Hey, but what does humping take? It happens by itself. But we are obsessed with frigging bigtime.' Mahesh.

Mahesh has been in journalism for five years, yet his salary in hand is just 8500 rupees. One or two who came after him got 12,000. A Mumbai newspaper came out with a Pune edition, and many freshers started with 15,000. But Mahesh gets just 8500. But a good thing that happened was that he could buy a 350 square feet place with his father's money at Bibvewadi. 'So my humping issue has been resolved,' Mahesh said laughingly when his marriage was fixed.

Mahesh doesn't even talk about a pay hike now. Some people get more salary, some people get less salary. Some people get salary hikes, some people don't get salary hikes. Nothing much to say there. Even if money is important, what is there to say? It's not as if those who have it say they have it, and those who don't have it say they don't have it. Mahesh however says it. Since his marriage he started taking a single vada in his vada sambar for snacks. 'Haven't got the money to have a full plate. I'll settle for single.' And when it's someone else paying, he takes double vada and says, 'I'm taking double because you are paying.' He's been with this paper for three years. Earlier, he was in reporting for a year. Now he's been on the desk for two years. Stating that he can't handle translation, they've put him on the district pages. And in truth, he does this work with great application. From the messed up faxes of district news to the making of the page, he deals with everything.

Office was fun. But the room wasn't bad either. In the room opposite his in the three-room flat lives Uday from Bihar, doing law. He almost never steps out of the room. Stays put inside. Has fun. Plays songs on the laptop sometimes, downloads whatever pictures he wants. Creates a fake profile on Facebook, deletes it. Chews gutka and keeps spitting it out from the gallery attached to his room. When the old woman from the neighbourhood comes up for a spat, says sorry, and for a full week, instead of spitting it out from the gallery, spits inside. Bathes when he can. Does as much cooking as possible on the stove – from Maggi to chicken. Ask him any time what's going on, the laughing response is, 'Having fun, comrade.'

Once Uday brought a black T-shirt. On the chest was a large sketch of Che Guevara. And on the back it said, 'Che the Comrade'. The T-shirt disappeared. Then Uday downloaded and saw the movie *Motorcycle Diaries*. He didn't want much to do with the original book. Didn't want to go that far. But said, 'Seems he was a good man.'

A reader has called Che Guevara a blood thirsty Satan in the letters column of *The Economist*. This really wasn't necessary. But it's okay. *Economist* was a newspaper too at the end of the day, appearing weekly. 200 rupees for a slim volume. Don't know how many copies are sold at the stall at 'Goodluck' square. But one copy arrives without fail at the library, in a white wrap.

The Economist – Time – Saadhana – Outlook – India Today – Newsweek – Frontline – Samaaj Prabodhan Patrika – Arthbodh Patrika – Seminar – National Geographic – many such mags. Those who read, read. Those who don't, don't. It's not because there is a library, but one could say that there is a connect between journalism and reading. There is no meaning in saying this, but Dasnurkar says this.

Whatever it be, all this stuff would come to the library and get piled up. That Che Guevara abusing issue of some week or the other in one of those monsoon months of 2008. The stuff would all pile up. Some would get disposed of later as waste-paper too, maybe. Some people would slip some of the stuff out of the library and take it home. The leftovers just collected dust in the library.

But it's good. All this library dust and the rest of it all, it's good. Meaning, all these *Economist* and *Time* and these other guys report one side of the story. Or all this printed stuff, they all, each one has its own bias, really. The library, however, is quiet.

The sleep that you get in the library, with the head resting on the cuddapah, is quite relaxing. Or just leaning the head back on the chair, that's relaxing too. All told, really relaxing.

So many come and go. Some stay in journalism, some don't. How many would have gone, where, there's no measuring it. Get themselves registered for alumni meet, so utterly casual and trivial. There are those select few who stay in focus. Where do the rest go? Those that get connected through the internet get connected. But what about the rest? Some of them have it in them to settle somewhere or the other in journalism and yet they don't settle. Some don't get the opportunity. Some others are not interested in settling here.

Ramchandra Parab too, after finishing this course, got into Library Science at the university. Thus got a place to stay too, the hostel facility. Enough and more have buggered journalism, Ramchandra declared, and went over. And when he met Ramchandra next, Ramchandra began with 'You...journalists!'

He asked Ramchandra, 'Why library science?'

'Arey brother, there's scope there too.'

'Don't want to get into a paper?'

'What kind of guys these paper guys are! You know it all, don't you? What do I say?'

'Say what you know.' He.

'Don't give enough money. No interest left, really.'

'Less money. Okay, one reason. What else?'

'What, what else, pal? You know it all.'

Some things everybody knows, but nobody talks about. Some things only a few know, but none among them talk about. For some, such things are not to be talked about. There are others who are just not interested in getting into this or that or any other thing. Then those whom people consider intellectuals, and those that are themselves 'The People'. So there are all these guys. In all this, somewhere in the middle of this mess, would be a rare few like Karle. There were a few more of them scattered here and there. Let them be, poor souls.

And where was he in the midst of this mess? He was having tea with Ramchandra in the open-air canteen at the university. Different kinds of chairs and tables – plastic and steel – spread out under the enormous banyan tree. They sitting on a ledge on the other side. What else Ramchandra would become by taking admission into Library Science, don't know, but two more years of coming over to have tea under this tree here, not bad at all. As they sat with their tea, a girl in a tight-fitting white T-shirt crossed the girls' hostel to the left. On the iron bench next to them sat an Iranian boy smoking a cigarette. Next to him was a red-lipped Iranian girl, light-haired, big long black jacket, buttoned right up.

Beyond them, near the xerox shop, stood a dark, sad girl in a blue Punjabi dress, stooping slightly with a sack on her shoulder. Here in front people sat eating–drinking–talking–laughing–walking. The rest scattered all over.

Right behind where he and Ramchandra sat, green, green, green trees, one inside the other. Real cool.

Four

He was making the page. The third page of the Pune supplement of the paper. A vertical double-column band of 'In Brief' on the left. He had to give small headlines for the news items for that band, and put them in. For the rest of the page, he had finished making a deck below a four-column item and a double-column item. Some people believe that a sub-editor's work is important, and work accordingly. Some others have worked and worked and are so sick and tired of it that they just drudge on.

Every news item needs to be read before it is laid into a page. Every news item needs to be edited. The matter is not to be expanded or condensed. The heading should be solid – such and other rules Karle observed. Did it to the best of his abilities. This is not possible for everyone, though. How much would Mahesh Kadam want to do for 8500? This work is never noticed, so people don't benefit. But there are people who do it all the same.

Sometimes he does observe Karle's rules. Some page number three or so of some blighted supplement, and some news item of 50–60 words there. Some story of a heart operation of some sort of a very small child, it seems. Appeal for financial help. Now this bald man in an ash-coloured shirt and black trousers comes to the office. The chief sub of that supplement was Tambe. He takes the man out for tea. Comes back in 15 minutes and says, 'This man has been coming for 13 years. The appeal that was put in yesterday for financial help, remember? So fifty rupees he gives every month, selects whichever appeal for help attracts him, and gives money to them. Jadhav is his name. Just an ordinary security guard, you know.'

How many want fame, how many don't want fame, how many get fame, how many don't get fame. There was intense darkness in intense dazzle.

And the second-hand bookseller at Lakdi Pul had gathered his books and was preparing to leave, while he sat on the ledge.

The second-hand bookseller sits at his spot, at around five in the evening with his books laid out on the empty space at Lakdi Pul. He stays there till eight-thirty or nine. Sudhakar brings his books in four or five cotton bags and lays them out on a plastic sheet. There are two stone benches in the open space, like the ones in gardens and all, bent inwards in the middle. The ledge nearby. A few bushes there. Behind that and below, the Vitthal temple. Next to it a massive peepal tree.

Sudhakar spreads his books out on the empty space and either sits or stands at the spot. Mechanical Engineering –

Java Script – C Language – HTML – Electronics – Sohoni Marathi-English Dictionary – Baba Kadam – Franz Kafka – Arthur Hailey – V.S. Naipaul – *National Geographic* – *Time* – *Deepavali* – *Mauj* – *Aawaaz* – Baburao Arnalkar – *Readers' Digest* – Gurunath Naik – *Newsweek* – Charles Dickens – Narayan Dharap – *War and Peace* – *Lateral Thinking* – *Masturbation: Bane or Boon* – *The Idiot* – *Crime and Punishment* – *How to Become a Billionaire* – Maxim Gorky – Italy – *Lokmanya Tilak Charitra* – *The Godfather* – Gogol – Manohar Malgonkar – Nostradamus – Swami Vivekananda – Karl Marx – Surendra Mohan Pathak – *The Age of Reason* – *Animal Farm* – *Seven Habits of Highly Effective People* – Jayant Narlikar – *The Outsider* – Swatantryaveer Savarkar – *How to Love and be Loved* – *Champak* – *Vedic Mathematics* – Babasaheb Ambedkar – Rabindranath Tagore – all these books sit stoically in front of Sudhakar.

He was sitting on the ledge while Sudhakar was gathering his books. To the left was a bunch of oldies. Very few people otherwise. Vehicles from here to there, there to here, there to there. Lines of red lights streaming. On the right, a big white light on an advertisement poster. Neon sign colours there. Bang in front, the 'Amul' advertisement done by Nandu painter. A girl in tight jeans with headphones was crossing the road. The oldies' group got up and drifted towards the right. A motorcyclist vroomed along Karve Road with the silencer missing. A fine-bosomed girl dressed in pink was now crossing the road there. Sudhakar and his rags-clad helper left their spot with their bag of books. A bright red light flashed alongside Karve Road. The girl in pink, walked past him, dupatta fluttering. She went in the direction of Tilak Road.

Ashen clouds on black sky.

He on the empty ledge.

To go to his building he had to move in the same direction that the girl had taken. But he didn't want it to seem like he was stalking her, so he hung around a bit longer and left after ten-fifteen minutes. Myriad coloured lights glittered in the black water of the river down the bridge. The cold wind was soft. The girl in pink on the way back. Fiddling with the mobile. Pink dress fluttering in the wind, white, tight-fitting leggings, black purse. Crossed him and disappeared somewhere behind him. Here, in front, the square.

He is standing near the police station. Kelkar Road approaches from the left past the footwear shops. Alongside it is Lakshmi Road; Next, from Senapati Bapat's statue, begins Kumthekar Road. To the right from here, all Lakdi Pul, Vitthal Temple on the other side. Next, Alka Talkies. Attached to that, Shastri Road. Liquor shops, xerox stores, and abutting that, Tilak Road, all of it. The square at the centre. The soft wind was cold.

Where the vehicles were coming from, where the horns were blowing from, where the lights were coming from, and where all of them together were going, he just didn't understand. He crossed the square nevertheless. On the other side of the huge glass pane at Regal restaurant, a girl wearing a deep-necked violet shirt was flashing her pearl-white teeth at a boy in a white shirt. The chain round the neck was rocking. Below the golden line, a dark upright tunnel inside. Laughing. Hair flying.

The vehicles standing at the signal. He walking down Tilak Road. A TV showroom at the left. An old hag sitting in front, scratching her head. A lane from there to the right goes towards Shastri Road. Here to the left a lane goes to Kumthekar Road.

He felt a terrible dizziness hitting him. Realizing that, he immediately moved to a side and stood holding on to whatever touched him. Massive sledge-hammers operating inside his head. A low tin-shed shack selling sugarcane juice, so he sat. One full. Oh bloody shit! Leaned his head on the table, but the hammering didn't stop. It was more painful at the back, so he leaned back, no relief. The juice arrived. One swig, and the hammers turned to gongs. Saw the yellow light in front. Some more juice and the gongs turned to cymbals. Saw the squeezed cane stick in front. There was a chunk of ice and a bit of juice in the glass. Finished the juice, sucked at the ice cube. He got off the blue painted wooden bench, five bucks at the counter, and out he came. The wind was cold and soft.

He came home and hit the cot. After the cane juice, he didn't have his meals. But that was all right. Everything else now was quiet. Very quiet. Uday was busy with something behind closed doors. You could see the tubelight peeping out from the edges of the door. The Bengalis had still not come. He was in there with the doors closed. Not one of these colossal things would appear in the newspapers tomorrow. No mistake there. Meaning, nothing newsworthy had happened really. But one can never be sure. News can spring out of anywhere. But even if it springs out of anywhere, it cannot spring out of very deep. Efforts however continue.

Dog biting man is not news, but man biting dog is news – people say rather glibly. But the fact is that dog biting man is what really gets circulated as news. For one, stray dogs are a major menace in the city. For another, there are people who feed such dogs. One of them had some kind of a firm or the other that sat in some multiplex and collected donations. So the issue was: however much someone says that dog biting man is not news, the fact is that these are the kinds of stories that become news. Easy to read, easy to digest, a good crap next morning.

But if it actually happened that a man bit a mangy dog near the market, who would get into the hassle of a news item, chyaayla? It would be all right as fun for a day. But by and large it is the dog that bites man, and that's what makes news. And if dog bites man, that's bad anyway. And it should become news. So it's all right.

Now all these musings make the head properly heavy. They did tire his head and pushed him into sleep mode. The tummy was protesting but the sleep in the head won.

He slipped into peaceful slumber. When the head crosses a certain limit, peaceful slumber results.

Dog, man, news, the whole stuff got to be a bit much, he felt, getting up next morning. But what can you say for the head? Lets everything in. But all in all, he felt better in the morning. The *Times of India* lay in front of Uday's door, he took it for the photographs. 'When the internet gets boring, this is good to have in hand.' It was now seven-thirty. Another three-four hours for Uday to get up, easily. So he brought the paper over to his room. There were no photographs, and there never is anything to read, so he put the paper back outside. Then he thought he should check out Laxman's cartoon. But what's so great there either? So he came back and just lay on the cot.

It was a really peaceful morning. November of 2009.

He had lived through exactly the same kind of time in the November of 2008, he felt. The same heaviness of head. Seven-thirty. Brushed his teeth and brought the paper in, put it back outside, missed the cartoon. Stretched out. A cold wind drifted in from the window. Every bit identical. Felt like it was a replay of the earlier event. But it was a good time, that. It was cold. The sun at the window. The light floods the entire room at this time of the morning.

A bed bug had slipped out of the cot and was crawling along the right wall. Then the smell of food cooking wafted in through the window.

Wanted something to eat.

But he didn't stir out. Switched on the FM on his mobile and just lay on.

Masakkali…masakkali… When he heard this popular song playing softly in the library, it was around three-thirty or four. When he entered, a pretty, dusky girl was sitting peacefully on the chair at the cuddapah, reading a newspaper, twirling a gold bangle with her left hand. Yellow, sleek dupatta, sunlit hair, both flying in the breeze from the fan above. The song playing on the mobile in front. Her back against the wooden chair. Eyes locked on the newspaper. Quiet library.

Right at the other corner a person with rather thick

spectacles sleeping, head resting on the cuddapah. Another person next to him in the same state.

When, instead of proceeding inside he came out, he saw a man in blue trousers and white shirt standing against a thick, round stone pillar, telling Dasnurkar, 'Prakash Paranjape is a maadarchod.' Shoe-flower shrub nearby.

Prakash Paranjape was a prominent editor. Age, reputation, friends, foes – the usual stuff that goes with prominence – he had.

The blue-trousered man talking to Dasnurkar pulled out two or three pages from the bag on his left shoulder. Xeroxes. Dasnurkar laughed and said, 'Arey, that's the kind they are.'

'No, wait, I'll show you the actual proof.' Man.

The man was saying interesting stuff, he thought, so as he stepped out of the library, he stopped close to where those two were talking.

Paranjape had addressed journalism students at the Working Journalists' Union, five months earlier. The man showed the xerox of the coverage of that lecture in Paranjape's own paper. 'The market for Marathi newspapers is set to increase in the future,' read the first sentence. Then the important role of technology, its impact on newspapers, the newly literate public that would emerge as readers – the news item covered this sort of stuff and whatever else Paranjape had blabbered. Dasnurkar saw the xerox. He saw it too.

The man then handed over the second xerox, two pages. There was an interview of Paranjape in an English fortnightly, ten days ago. He had stated there that the newspaper he edited would disappear in twenty years. He had said further, 'In fact there will be no Marathi paper. There may be pamphlets or something; people will speak Marathi, but the newspaper will not be viable. Economics and culture must match.' Just so that it shouldn't appear that he was quoting sentences out of context, the man showed the entire xeroxes of both the news item and interviews. Direct evidence.

'Arey bastard, go fuck your mother there if you want to. But why mislead new kids? Market for Marathi! Bloody bastard!' Man on fire.

Dasnurkar laughed. He watched.

'Meet him direct, shouldn't you, and tell him. Let him know,' Dasnurkar said.

'Did that, didn't I? Mailed him twice, "Dear sir" and all that. But where's the reply? What I have to say is, all your other monkey business is all right, your political inclinations one can understand. But, wretched bastard, why dupe new kids? And these bloody idiots call him the last in the glorious tradition of Marathi editors!' Man aflame.

'Let go, re. This is old stuff among these guys.' Dasnurkar.

'Exactly! That's why it's important to target the arch crook. Get after everyone, and your brains will drain out.' Man aflame laughed.

Dasnurkar laughed. He laughed.

'This too, chyaayla, people would call naiveté. The rest is okay, sir, we don't ask for a moral spring-cleaning of journalism. Not even possible. And people may do all that on their own. But these fuckers duping new kids, that's not right. That's why, sir, I ask you to display these xeroxes on the notice board.' Man aflame.

Dasnurkar took the xeroxes. His ability to hear a person out is sometimes immense. He understood the blue-trousered gent. Didn't call on the weight of his own experience to think blue-trousers a chootiya. In this entire mess, how much, after all, would be the overall significance of the difference between what Prakash Paranjape said in the lecture and in the interview? And there was nothing new anyway in this kind of bogusness. Blue-trousers very likely knew it too. But he held that new kids shouldn't lose out.

Dasnurkar left with the blue-trousered gent. He then felt like returning to the library. Before getting into the inner passage he sat on the chair at the pink sunmica table. It was snooze time, so he rested his head automatically on the table. The 4 o'clock light streamed in silently from the window. The song on the mobile seemed to have gone, very likely.

Five

'Talks of moral-immoral are a lot of hogwash. What's happened is that earlier people knew the difference between them and made their choices. But a majority of kids these days don't even know the difference, so what choices are they going to make, bhenchod?' When in the mood, Karle has abuses for snacks with his tea.

Karle downs loads of tea. The tea-man near the office really makes fabulous tea. Once the steam gets into the eyes, you are bound to feel a little tranquil. With every hot sip, more and more tranquillity. Karle and he are out for their daily cup. Behind Karle sits a dark woman. Green blouse and glossy black back visible. Hair absolutely sleek, braided. Opposite her sits a dark, broad-faced man in a soiled white shirt. Don't know what they are talking about. He doesn't know their language. One may guess it's Kannada, but he doesn't know the subject of their conversation.

'The example of Paranjape is very trivial. Cases of being

suckered have been around for very long. Most people earlier stayed conveniently quiet, but the kids of today, it doesn't even occur to them that they are being suckered. Just a lot of brainless enthusiasm.' Karle dunked another abuse in his tea.

If people like Paranjape are representative, he doesn't know what people like Karle are. Karle's name doesn't often appear in the papers, and he doesn't get enough opportunities to write either. 'Opportunities are not given, they are created.' He does not have to hear this philosophy because he has now been working for 14 years. The Journalism course teaches that the sub-editor is the spine of a news organization. Karle may very likely be the spine or he may not, but instead of getting into this intellectual discussion, it's better to down another cup of tea, so he finished off the second cup that Karle had ordered.

Karle paid twenty bucks for the four teas on leaving. The dark woman had beautiful, sad, limpid eyes, but Karle's attention wasn't towards her. Why was the man in front of her looking down? She was looking out somewhere else. Her entire face was beautiful. She sat with the pallu of her sari tucked, the man in front sat staring at the floor, and Karle and he stepped out.

The old cardboard man's addiction to tea is of almost Karle-esque proportions. His and the old man's tea timings are not fixed. But even so, they run into each other at the same spot at the same time a few times a week. When the mood is upon him, Karle talks during tea; but the old man – never.

The old man works. His face never shows any tension of

his tattered trousers. He doesn't bend under the weight of so many staring eyes. Doesn't fluster looking at women. But looks at them when in the mood. He doesn't mind people, people don't mind him. But the old man is not a poor cow. A cow's eyes are moist, the old man's dry. The old man doesn't sit by the road, doesn't lie by the roadside. He is either searching for stuff he wants, or snoozing on an iron bench at the bus-stop on Bajirao Road, or drinking tea, or sitting peacefully on the stone ledge reading *Navaa Kaal*.

The acquaintance between him and the old man is the kind that develops when people keep seeing each other day after day. Once, he was having paani-poori by the roadside at Appa Balwant Chowk. The Rajasthani paani-poori kid, smaller than his stall, gave him his last piece. He asked for a masala-poori when he saw the old cardboard man coolly passing by. With a gesture of the hand he asked the old man whether he would like to join in. The old man shook his head. The old man was tough. The old man was rough. But for whatever it was worth, with these occasional crossings on the road, he drew support from the old man.

At 7 o'clock of the darkening evening, there were so many lights, colours, vehicles, shops glittering along the road. There were so many sounds: mobiles, people, vehicles. But the old man in his dusty, dark-blue T-shirt and trousers walked tension-free along the road.

On another occasion in the past: so many lights, colours, vehicles, glittering shops. So many sounds: mobiles, people, vehicles. He and Ramchandra were having paani-poori at FC Road. Ramchandra said, 'Bugger it all, There's no hope for us.' This was Ramchandra as second year was coming to an end.

For the rest, FC Road was as it had always been. A crowd of bosoms, buttocks, thighs. Vehicles. Arcade panes. And dark, thin, naked kids on the divider. Clothes shops. Soft, full bosoms showing a bit. Pink elastic peeping from beneath the T-shirt. Selling letter-blocks strung into bracelets on the footpath outside Wadeshwar restaurant, her dirty green pallu on her head, sat the dusky woman, fair-thighed girls beyond. There those green trees. Here this coffee. Plumbline-straight hair on fair and dusky backs. Wretched bloody divider and he crunch-gulping paani-poori.

When the vehicles stop at the red signal, the kids get off the divider and beg. Or when on the footpath, they beg.

The editor called the low-salaried ones to his cabin and said, 'During my time I have worked for fifty bucks a month. You have this opportunity, put it to use. Don't sit crying. I was married and the paper I was working for closed down. Married, with a two-year-old boy. And no job. You can't even imagine the condition I was in. Spent six months in this condition. Then finally I got another job. Reached here by climbing the ladder by slow degrees. We alone can help ourselves. Nobody else can. The opportunity you have, the brand name, use it. We ourselves should project our own selves. It's important to get joy out of work. I reach here at eleven in the morning. Why? Because I enjoy it here. I tell my boy the same thing. You do theatre, right? Do it. But you should get pleasure out of doing it. He has now decided to make a career on stage. I told him go, go with pleasure. Our fields give us opportunities to enrich ourselves, so take them.

See how you can increase the store of your knowledge.'

Stupid bloody idiot. Head exploding, yet the meeting doesn't wind up. Just thought, couldn't voice it though. He and Mahesh exchanged looks of disgust, but the editor went on rambling, spouting his lies.

'And keep this in mind, time keeps changing forever. Your salary may suddenly shoot up tomorrow. Till then, make use of the opportunity you have. Our work should be in good order. No one should lift a finger at it. Look at me, everything authentic. Speak openly, keep the heart clean.'

The editor went on for almost an hour.

He and Mahesh had once hatched a plan of laughing loudly at anything the editor said. Whenever he began, and went past a couple of sentences, laugh loudly – ha hahahahahaha! What other remedy? Just laugh loudly. Doesn't cost money.

Uday and he burst into laughter.

Now, whenever Uday makes a new dish, he calls him over. Brings an old or new movie, and calls him over. Talks a lot. No tension. Has a law firm back home in Patna. 'If I really have no tension, where do I fetch it from, comrade?' he says. Once he brought a small book for learning Marathi. Then any time they crossed, he would ask, 'Kasa'ye saaheb?' (How are you, sir?)

Once he played a song for him on his laptop and asked casually, 'Comrade, have you heard this song?'

Kaal se pehle wahee tha – kaal ke baad wahee
Jaaney kitni sadiyon se – le rahaa voh teri
Teri teri teri teri
Teri teri teri teri

Gaand mein danda re – teri gaand mein danda re
Naa baans ki bansi na soney ka sariya
Gaand mein danda re

The song came to this point and he and Uday started laughing. Uncontrollably!
'Listen further, listen further.'

Aayaa thha voh XL mein – sapnon ka ek baadal
IR ki ladki hot bahut thhi –
Mann mein machee thhi halchal
Saath jiyenge saath padhengey –
Saath chalengey paidal
Pataa chala par bike vaala koyi –
Ley gayaa usko aa kar
Gaand pe pad gayee laat –
Toh tootaa sapnon ka mahal

Now he and Uday really held their sides and started roaring. The song went on with more of the same kind of stuff. They listened and they roared with insane laughter. Their eyes streamed. Uday was exhausting himself rolling on the cot. Then he deliberately slipped on the floor and started rolling there, hand on tummy. Went on saying, 'Isn't it true, comrade, isn't it true!'

Six

State Assembly elections – October 2009. Thickset MLA Saheb sat on the sofa in his vest, lungi hitched up and feet in warm water. He sat opposite, pad and pen in hand. Just a touch nippy. The work? Oh just a 15-minute interview. The paper would publish the interview and the MLA would buy the number of copies pre-arranged with the Marketing Department. The work was straight and simple, and the interview was just propaganda. The ochre mark the MLA carried on his forehead all day was missing. The MLA said: 'Yaa, hullo. We've brought out a manifesto, and you'll get everything there. Something to eat?'

The transport issue, wayside hawkers, beedi workers, health facilities for senior citizens, what new to expect?

Soft sofa, two glass showcases, big teapoy, idli-sambar, cold drinks.

'Should read well, understand? Otherwise the journalist kids these days are not even worth a look, literally. I say this because it's you. Hey there, you, go drop this gentleman. See you then. Call any time,' smiled the MLA.

The MLA's interview was published a couple of days later.

❖

'Tell me, did they realize it was paid news because the article appeared in the English paper?'

'We have an absolutely open package at our place.'

'Yes, but the same article was published in two Marathi papers under different bylines. And yet you need a Tamil journalist from an English newspaper to say this? The kinds of chootiyas you chaps are, pal!'

'It's just that there would be some discussion regarding journalism under the excuse of elections. Nothing new here. What new stuff did he say?'

'He said something, didn't he, even if nothing new? You wretched bastards, do you ever even talk about old things?'

'What woolly-headedness, pal!'

'The issue is not whether we can do something or not. But whatever is happening, whether we at least accept that or not, that's the issue. All these oil companies shove the stick up America, and then America gets busy shoving it up the oil countries. Can we do anything at all about it? No, we can't. But at least those who know about it talk, don't they? So the sticks that are being shoved up yours, talk about them too, at least some time. Talk at least when it is possible to do so.'

'Go ask your district newsmen what paid news is.'

'This money exchanging hands, it's old stuff. But happening straight up there at the organizational level is a bit serious.'

'Lay your pages properly, put your news properly, and let

the world go fuck its mom!'

Paid news got talked about for a couple of months or so. The P. Sainath article appeared in the *Hindu*. And then, endless debates. Debates within debates. Debates on debates. Debates under debates. Debaters, all. Karle – Mahesh – he – Tambe – Sarmalkar, Malusare – chief reporter, cheap reporter – other reporters – Ranade – Bhosale – resident editors – editors – TV channels. Clamour round the clock. Debate inside a debate, with tea, with sips, with snacks. Debates flaunting a hundred opinions after reading just a booklet, gabbing on for six months after reading just a book, honest opinions and dishonest opinions after reading nothing, oldies with dishonest opinions after reading quite a bit. A proper diarrhoea of brainless blabber. You've read this, you've read that? This is rubbish, that's conjecture. Hyaanchya aaycha! Empty debates on full bellies. The filthy, filthy, filthy stench of rotting intellectuality.

The three-legged dog lay fuck-the-world peaceably, soaking up the sun, and seeing that made him feel nice. Very nice. There was no point in over-sentimentality, a dog doesn't do that. No point in over-enthusiastic dumbness, a dog doesn't do that either. October 2008 coming to an end. It was cold. Twelve-thirty in the afternoon. On the left turn after crossing the thick stone pillar corridor, the door to the library; the office right there in front. This little square patch out here, where the corridor ends, has remained open at the top. An office window opens there out of the stone wall. An open patch, roughly 20 by 20 square feet. Sunlight streams in from above. The branches of the gulmohar out there on the other side spread out a little bit. Their twigs, small yellow-green leaves fall on the square. It gets rains during the monsoons. It's a little cool there during the summer, and a little warm during the winter.

The three-legged dog sat so beautifully in the stone square, peaceably taking in the sun. He never even barked. Never seen loitering outside the department premises. His food needs are met within the premises. Doesn't piss around pointlessly all over. He would of course be making a trip out some time or the other to relieve the organ under his tail, that's it. Otherwise there's nothing to match the dog's peaceableness. Discussions, tichya aayla, could go climb a tree, the dog would have none of it.

The dog's connect with the library too is to the extent of sleeping. He sleeps under the cuddapah.

He walks into the library. Inside, to the right, in a glass cupboard, is a blue-bound volume with 'M.N. Roy' embossed on it, cover missing. Its place never shifts, just adequate to be noticed, and it sits there, quiet. On it today rests Sanjay Sangvai's *The River and Life*, in a blue cover. Figures – issues – Narmada River – dam. To its right is some or the other book on communication theory, with the name written vertically in illegible letters. There's a massive jumble of these books in the cupboard. But there are other books too besides these, pulled out here and there from the heap. *India: A Million Mutinies Now*, V.S. Naipaul, sat in the left corner of the bottom shelf, and in one of its middle chapters the Namdeo Dhasal of the earlier days said, who is this jenny-ass named freedom? Actually, Fidel Castro's little *My Early Years* is there too. So what's there to its being there? Anything can be anywhere. The introduction to *Early Years* is by Marquez of *One Hundred Years*. On the pink sunmica table in front are *Loksatta* and *Asian Age* next to each other.

He picked up the two papers and entered. There were other papers there lying on the cuddapah that the others had brought in earlier, some neatly folded, some in a mess. For the rest, there was nobody else inside. He sat. A strange light from the window in front, the trees swaying outside. A little gust of wind, and the paper in the corner on the verge of falling fell. The cobwebs along the window wiggled. The sunlight wiggled. A little cold.

There were no photographs worth noticing in the supplement of the *Asian Age*. He put the paper down. The library was in a stupor. Good. Out on the other side, in front, beyond the trees the green creepers spread over the wires. His head was aching a bit. Jayesh Shinde peeped in, and left with a wave of hand. He felt tired. The stomach was aching a bit. He put his head on the cuddapah. His own legs below and the rough tiles. Dust. He would throw up, felt he, felt the head and felt the stomach. He felt listless. Got up, and somehow made his way to the toilet there – some kind of basin they've fixed there – and retched. Gurgled, retch-retch-retched. Coughed. Flushed. Coughed. Spat. Flushed again. Eyes watery. Hrrumped. Spat. Flushed again. Clear water inside the white commode. No splashes anywhere. Good. He felt better. Washed his face in the big basin there. Scrubbed himself. Blew his nose. Did his hair. Wind across the window. In the mirror in front, the nose looked a little red. Mopped the face with a handkerchief. A little nippy.

The head cool. Pushed the door and stepped out. Felt like sleeping. Lovely wooden window on the left with a thick mesh screen, partition sheet on the right, he stepped in. Big wooden table. Sat in the ancient armchair in front.

Out there in the library is a passage fitted with cuddapah for sitting. That and this small room inside. The fricking fan here, the last time it conked off, it remained conked off. This wooden armchair here is good. He slept off. Got to rest his head. Everything went really, really quiet. Good he got to rest his head. Really good. He slept.

Despite the afternoon puke, he didn't skip Lakdi Pul. Sudhakar sat with his books spread out in front of him. Vehicles moved from here to there, there to here. The old cardboard man too would surely have done his crossword and left before Sudhakar arrived. The fine-bosomed girl of the pink dress now passes this way almost every day. Today, the dress is moss-green, yellow leggings tight-fitting as before. A mobile at her ear today right from the time she crossed. Moved in that direction.

Rafeeq came from this direction. He was sitting on the ledge, and waved his hand. Rafeeq waved his right hand; his left hand is limp. Rafeeq came to join the journalism course from Kerala. In the early days, he was at least a little bit in the flow; but later, once he got out, he remained out. Back to Kozhikode after the course. Rafeeq smiled with his big teeth and sat alongside him on the ledge. 'Arey, this room is also bad,' he said in half English. 'Bed bugs are sucking my blood.' Full-sleeved blue shirt, hands folded, the left hand held in the right one as always, he sat on the ledge. During the second year of the second semester Rafeeq started staying on cot basis in Deccan. Then got into the habit of visiting Lakdi Pul. Lately, however, he's not seen much, just about anywhere. Browsed through the books for five or ten minutes and left.

All these people who have drifted in different directions are bound to be located somewhere. Some or the other of them would also be doing well. Some or the other would be doing bad too.

Rafeeq had started a blog and put up a post. He had written that his mother and some other girl were the two women in his life. Rafeeq told him, so he read it. Didn't know whether anybody else had also read. Some or the other person would surely have read. Comments zero. Even so, Rafeeq should have continued with the blog. Would have created some kind of record, to whatever extent. Social networking afterwards, full of fake profiles of real people; he saw Rafeeq's profile too there, but it didn't carry any meaning. The daily social falsehoods on Facebook, the world so lovely lovely, events every day, claps please! New place, stories old. Tomorrow, at another new place, the stories continue to be old, there wasn't any point in spending any further time on it. So many books in the market talking about so many points. One such, titled *Fakebook Generation*, was sold by Sudhakar to someone just the other day right here for a hundred rupees.

The hundred rupee note blew away. Wind wind. A really mild wind arrived. The note stopped, recovered. Strong wind. Monstrous roar. October of 2008 coming to a close. Wind cold. The plastic under the books fluttered, but didn't blow away, stayed. Trees bent. Wind humungous. Who are we to stand up to it? He stayed sitting on the ledge.

2009

17 cops martyred in Maoist attack

Gadchiroli, 8 October: Seventeen policemen lost their lives in the armed Naxal attack on Laheri Police Station in taluka Bhamragadh today (Thursday). A total of 51 policemen have died in similar such attacks since January.

Village Laheri is situated 31 kilometres from Bhamragadh on the Bhamragadh-Vinagunda road. The Naxals mounted an attack on a police squad that was on patrol duty near the Laheri police station. Among those martyred were ten constables of the C60 Special Police Force as well as a Police Inspector. Investigation into the killings has begun in full earnest in the area.

Seven

I honestly don't know exactly when he started considering himself useless. Even if I had known, I would probably not have talked about it. But honestly, honestly, I don't know. Basically I don't even know why he started considering himself useless.

But what would one do merely sitting in the open-air canteen? So suggested we took a round. But he was so awfully exhausted. He was sitting on the iron bench next to the xerox guy. Tired. Elevated road in front. Crowds here. He was pooped out. But I said to him let's go, bored of warming our butts pointlessly sitting, chyaayla. Must have been hungry, so had upma and tea, seven and three, ten bucks. After the first mouthful of upma he felt better. Hmm.

He downed another two-three mouthfuls with chutney quite easily. Water.

Gave him a glassful of water. Emptied it down his throat. Tea.

Hmm.

Felt like he was let out of prison. The tea was hot. The steam before the eyes, felt like there was steam everywhere. The tea was seriously hot. Another. Three bucks in change.

The steam from the wonderful tea wafted up his face. Droplets formed on his brow and nose. Had tea. Saw the sunlight. Throat felt nice. Head felt nice.

Left the hubbub behind and set off from a back street.

Told him he should eat well.

He said yes.

Told him, 'What's to be done of the uselessness?'

He didn't say anything.

Chalo good, chyaayla. The ambience wasn't right either for talking. On the left, the sun going right lateral. Slanting yellow rays beaming. On the right, the dark of the green trees. What, after all, does one say in these conditions? So he stayed shut, and I didn't ask him. Spotted Sayli Jadhav and Jayesh Shinde approaching. He started. They hadn't noticed first. Smiled when they saw us. He was rattled. Ellis Garden on the right. Canopy of trees. On a swing there, a very tiny girl in a checked uniform was cutting wild arcs. Stopped right in the middle. Then sat rocking gently. Sat taking soft swings in the slanting sun. Matched the shadow with her smile. Bold as the devil. Then ran to the woman sitting there with her satchel, and dissolved into her sari. Both smiled. He really felt very nice. Not a pinch of a lie here. He was tired, yes. But with the kind of happiness those two were soaked in, what was there to say? The kid held the woman's hand and walked away in the other direction with cocky steps.

He turned left. Looked back and noticed Sayli and Jayesh

had reached the open air canteen at a distance. Waiting by the vehicle.

The gravel path through the banyan in front. Shingled Lalit Kala Kendra to the left. Red bricks, cobbled stone pathway. Banyan tangled above. Or branches of the same banyan tangled this way and that. Up and down. Bunches thick and thin. Sun rays perfectly aslant. On the vertical branches and on the cobbled steps too. On the scattered leaves too. Yellow shadows falling over each other. Sunshine swaying on swaying branches. Sunshine spending itself out on the up and down stones of the cobbled steps.

The main university building in front. He turned right. A ledge climbing up to the left. A lawn in the middle. Then the main university building. Under repairs for three years. Crook, the Vice Chancellor. To the right down there, a tin shed. Tin rusted all over.

He felt nauseous. Aayla, what to do? There, to one side next to the tin sheet down there is a tap. He instantly retraced his steps. Throat ached horribly. Head exploded. He threw up. Threw up, he did. His ears burnt. Finally, a spot of red. A little bit of blood. Opened the tap. All gone. Disappeared. Clean. He was clean drained out. Splashed his face. But he was completely drained. Should stretch out nicely in the sun behind there near the tin sheet, he thought. Exhausted.

Thought he could go further up there and sit peacefully, so he set off, but someone was there on the ledge, legs folded, fiddling around with songs on the mobile. A mad hotch-potch of songs played fast backward and forward.

Hai guzaarish –
– hotthon sey chhoo lo tum
Jhonka havaa kaa aa –
– dil giraa daftan
– aajaa paas paas

He turned ahead. These flat tiles under the tin-shed instead of sand. He went further. A road down there on the right. Jayesh and Sayli passed him on their vehicle. Tiles finished. Now these few big stone steps. Road in front. He was flustered. Sat on the steps towards the back. To the left, a carpet of cork flowers.

Aaycha ghoda.

We were coming back home from office on a cold November night of 2009. He was near the City Post Office on Lakshmi Road at one-thirty at night. I asked him again, what's to be done about the uselessness. He got disgusted.

The women around there didn't look like women. Men looked like pricks. The rows of wood-planked shanties looked dilapidated. Lipsticks leaked. Mattresses mucked. Bosoms bled. Saris soiled. Tiles twisted. Lanes looped.

He crossed the square. Masseurs had hitched up their lungis and massaged bare backs, legs, scalps, slap–slurp–slap. Slapped thighs. Songs playing on a black radio. Nothing seemed to make any sense. Back there, at the square, a guy hit a woman at the nape of her neck. What could a person do? But she did something. She shoved the guy so hard that he went flying and landed at the closed shutter and lay sprawled against it. She tucked her pallu and left. A yellow bulb shone overhead.

He. The road here now was completely deserted. The crowd had been left behind. Except for an occasional guy driving pointlessly fast. He – road – beautiful yellow lights – closed shops – closed sky – and cold.

The road now moved straight, straight towards Lakdi Pul. The skeletal old kharvas seller was pushing his cart behind, tiny kerosene lamp dangling.

But he had to turn left to go to his room.

Lanes lanes lanes.

A security guard in a monkey cap sat on a chair in front of a white-lit ATM, legs stretched on another chair, arms folded, mobile playing a song – *Chhoo kar mere man ko kiya toone* –

Lanes lanes lanes.

Near the Maruti temple a sweater-clad old man in rags was talking to dumb dogs.

Wind blows wind.

Cold.

The tree leaves fluttered.

Lane to the room in front.

Building ahead.

Two flights up.

Left turn right turn.

Yellowed white door.

Lift the latch and in.

Dark passage ahead.

Unlock left.

He in his room.

Switched on tubelight, put mobile on table, and stretched out on the cot.

Hadn't passed out instantly. Mobile pinged. Message. Old friend. Sends at least a couple of messages a month. That's the only contact now. And doesn't just forward any old message. Sends only the good ones. Gives painting lessons. Does wall-painting. Passing acquaintance, but sends messages. And only when they are good.

So, thought for the day: 'An ant is tiny, but it can chew your butts. Can you chew its butts? No, right? So don't think less of anyone.'

He smiled and then he drifted off to sleep.

It was cold.

Eight

When Sachin Tendulkar hit 200, there was chaos in the office. The South Africans were sick. But the entire office looked agog at Sachin. There was hustle later for making the pages, but right then he was close to 200. So the pages would have to wait. Because Tendulkar was playing. The rest was beyond comprehension, but discussions there had frozen. People who speak against Tendulkar do, those who speak for him do, too. But it did happen that that day all discussion was spiked. No space for anything else. It was more or less certain too that the editorial next day would be on Sachin. The editor is a Sachin fan. The South Africans were sick and tired of bowling.

When India's score crossed 175, Sachin got his hundred off 90 balls. When Sachin reached 170, India had crossed 300. Those sitting below, close to the TV – which was on a stand fitted to the wall some 10 feet higher in the corner – were craning their necks to see Sachin. Some stood in the

middle of the room, some at the back. Those who blocked
the view, when told to move, would move. Then Dhoni
walked in at three down. About 40 overs had been bowled.
While all this was going on, Sachin reached 195. The highest
one-day score in 140 balls. 'And this happens to be Sachin
Tendulkar,' said the commentator. Then Mark Boucher
shook Tendulkar's hands. The India score then was 345. In
the middle of the 45th over. Then Dhoni started hitting and
time began running out for Sachin's 200. So much so that the
last over arrived. But when he scrambled for the single and
reached 200, it was bedlam. 'First man on the planet to reach
200, it's the superman from India.' There in the pavilion, Gary
Kirsten, Sehwag and the others were clapping and grinning.
Sachin peeled off his helmet, raised his arms and looked at the
sky. The entire stadium and the entire office were screaming.
He put on his helmet again. India's final score was 401.

This is how it happened. No spicing up here, no taking
sides, no discussions, no nothing. This is how it happened.

Many such stories.

Malusare versus Ranade Bhosale, Bhosale versus chief
reporter, chief reporter versus two junior reporters, a middle-
level reporter versus Ranade, Tambe versus junior reporter,
resident editor versus small fish, the real big fish of Mumbai
and biggish fish of Pune versus all other small fish, many small
fish versus each other, the big fish of Delhi versus whoever,
tichya aayla – all got drowned – because Mahesh Kadam
brought egg curry to celebrate Sachin's double hundred. When
eating this egg curry, it feels like pretty much nobody in the

world can make egg curry the way Mahesh's wife makes it. What it actually feels like, eating this egg curry, is impossible to express in words. No oil floating on the top doesn't mean that it's insipid, but not insipid doesn't mean that it's spicy hot. The taste rests beautifully somewhere in the middle. Taste that wouldn't disagree with anyone from anywhere – Vidarbha – Marathwada – Konkan – Western Maharashtra – anywhere else. Egg curry and chapatti. Everyone at the office loved it. Whoever ate it was sold. The fish versus fish game went hollow against half an hour of egg curry.

Half an hour on Lakdi Pul makes plenty of other things go hollow too. Sudhakar collects books from here and there during the day. Sits home in the afternoon and prices the books according to the worth of the book/writer. Lays them out here in the evening. Runs a household decently on this money. A wife, a girl in standard IX, another in standard VII, a boy in standard VI, this entire household runs on peddling books at Lakdi Pul. Amazing.

Balding, needing glasses for reading, Sudhakar is in his forties. He is as old as the number of years Sudhakar has been selling books at Lakdi Pul. He is touching 24. Sudhakar is touching 47. Till the kids are settled down, so for another 15 odd years, all this must go on for Sudhakar. Which means so many things going on must continue going on.

The place there on Lakdi Pul, the ledge for sitting on, people moving to and fro, people buying second-hand books ranging from *Masturbation: Bane or Boon* to *National Geographic* or to Dostoevsky, people willing to buy such and other books need to be there.

For the last 25 years, things have gone along well enough, even allowing for a few changes here and there. But there was no saying anything about things for the next fifteen. The speed was a littlebit–littlebit-littlebit much-much–much. But whatever happened, chyaayla, how much, after all, would it be?

Therefore, Sudhakar was smiling peacefully in front here and speaking his Kannada-perfect Marathi. Seeing that made him feel nice. For the rest, because the earth revolved around the sun, revolved around itself too. It was happening, then, that things were rolling along in their own orbits. For now, at least.

For now, at least, Sudhakar would surely see his family through. That was why, in the December of 2009, slippers on feet, clad in a loose, black, full-sleeve shirt, Sudhakar was smiling. He sat there absorbing all this.

The wind came, the wind moved on.

And from the right, the regular, the fine-bosomed girl with beautiful round buttocks wearing a tight-fitting yellow dress and tight-fitting white leggings showing her thighs crossed the road, speaking on her mobile.

He sat on the ledge.

Balasaheb Manvi seated on the bench. In the middle of December of 2008.

Balasaheb visited the bridge every evening. A big, white, full-sleeved shirt. Old steel watch, rubber slippers, spectacles, stubble, bald head, bony limbs, Balasaheb arrived hobbling at Lakdi Pul and sat on the stone bench. He had a hump. He sat exactly at the spot where the bench bent inwards, so he would likely have felt nice sitting there. He would cross over from the Karve Road side and come here and sit peacefully.

He would look at the books, but was never seen buying them. Would just pick one up sometimes and sit reading on the stone bench. But never seen buying one. Sometimes he made some kinds of jottings in his little diary.

Balasaheb's mouth was operated upon, don't know how far back. So one part of his face had caved in and looked weirdly thin. He had a problem speaking. He dripped saliva when he spoke, so he doesn't speak much on account of that. Not speaking much once, he had spoken about the operation.

While looking through the books, when he wanted to browse through one, he would squat on his haunches, bend double, raise the book close to his eyes and give it a minute look. The mouth quivered now and then. Once he picked up Arthur Hailey's Airport and looked at it for a long time. Then made a gesture to Sudhakar with his hand, indicating, 'How much?'

Sudhakar said – twenty-five

Balasaheb said – ten

– twenty-five

– fifteen

– twenty-five

– fifteen

– twenty-five

Then Balasaheb stayed quiet. Sudhakar generally brings the price down. But that again depends on his mood. Balasaheb skimmed through the book again, and then he got up. Got up and locking his hands behind his back, hobbled away towards Karve Road.

The wind came, the wind moved on.

It was cold.

Nine

Red-red arches, white-white, dirty, round-round pillars, stone-stone lovely walls, one-or-two, one-or-two low, stone steps. Glass-paned wooden windows, two panes smashed, one jackfruit tree standing erect, a small bush in the middle, a broken table there, a table here, not broken – the sight flustered him. It was either end of December 2008 or start of January 2009. The 3 p.m. sun.

He entered the classroom here on this side where Siddhesh Joshi sat on the first bench, flipping TV channels. The dusky girl here was reading some book or the other. There against the wall Ramchandra was just staring at the TV. The door in the other corner, permanently closed. The sun shone there on the cobwebs, the dust, the benches. He sat. TV in front.

Siddhesh put on *National Geographic* – a language dies every fortnight – endangered languages. Changed channel. Songs. Afternoon time, so stayed on that channel. Maayla, don't want any heavy stuff, said Siddhesh. That song again:

Masakkali masakkali. Next, suddenly, *Mera saayaa saath hoga*. Raise the volume, the girl told Siddhesh. The volume rose a bit. It was nice. Meanwhile, Jayesh Shinde came and stood at the door, looked around the room, and left. Somebody came in and sat at the last bench.

– *Mera kuchh saamaan* ...

Half an hour, 45 minutes just slipped away. Peacefully quiet. The ads between the songs went mute automatically. There were four-five people in the class then. It was a bit cold. All this was possible only on the department premises. Could swing it only in the journalism department. Something to do, maybe, with the stone building.

Hyaanchya aaichi gaand, said Mahesh Kadam when the news came that a builder had beaten up the president of the Journalists' Union. Entered his house and beat him up badly. Basically, a senior reporter of a big paper, and the president of the Journalists' Union on top of that. It was expected, then, that the issue would flare up, and flare up it did. Flared up proper. Bhosale said, 'I've just talked to the Home Minister's PA.' Every person had something or the other to say on this topic. Then the agitations to protest against the incident. Different kinds of campaigns stretched across four-five days on the whole. Silent March. Silent Chain. Sit-in, sometimes one, sometimes another. Every union member received SMS messages of the time and place of the campaigns. Journalists came to the appointed places too. Lectures on the need for laws to protect journalists. Protests. Whatever else seemed proper.

Assurance arrived, further action will be taken. Police, court, and the likes. In the middle of all this, another agitation somewhere. Big time discussions this time. And involving heavy weights too. The small fry had no other work beyond swelling a crowd.

'This time we mustn't let them go, re. I mean, this is just too much!' Tambe.

'And you know what? They have no fear of anything re. If we don't speak up now, this will become a norm, journalists too never speak,' Malusare.

'No, no. This time no letting them go. I've talked to Saheb,' Bhosale.

'What's this going on?' Sarmalkar.

'We'll make it real big. What do they think of themselves?' chief reporter.

'Basically I'm a person that has emerged from movements. Have been the president of the union, too. And this time there's no bloody stepping back. They have to be rattled. Arey, tomorrow you'll kill!' The editor lied again.

And nobody can say exactly when, but the whole thing just collapsed. Silent, absolutely. The entire issue drifted somewhere or the other. After all the song and dance and drama in the beginning, nothing at all came of it. And nobody let out a squeak. Well, everybody has a hundred things to do, y'know, so everybody got sucked back into his own stuff. The guy who was beaten up, he was the president of the union, wasn't he? For the rest, everything was as always.

'Can barely unite for four-five days, what union can they have, bhenchod?' said Karle once during tea. Otherwise, nobody said absolutely anything at all. Well, there would be some people somewhere or the other who would likely have said something of this kind. But nothing worth talking about.

The tree in the department premises fell on 20 January 2009. He was standing there, close to the other classroom. Siddhesh was there too. Plenty of people. At the Department of Foreign Languages. At the parking. At the canteen. In class. The crackling noise of the tree falling attracted the attention of a lot of people. Though it was in the parking area, it did not fall on any vehicle. Fell somewhere in the middle. So all vehicles had to drive around from the other side to access the parking lot. The tree lay there, green leaves, branches and all, for many days. Whatever trunk was blocking the passage was moved to a side. But the main trunk, roots and all, stayed right there. Later, in the next monsoons, it threw up new shoots. But it went, finally. Just a little stump stayed on for a long time.

What would remain here in 3009?

When this thought hit him, it ripped him apart. There was no point in lying. He had begun to realize his uselessness well before the tree fell. Nothing particular in that. But this, however, ripped him apart, big time.

That was when he felt the innumerable unbridled abuses of the Marathi tongue come to his aid. If nothing else, the market sank with the mouthing of abuses, and that was satisfaction enough.

He, of course, was very clearly not going to be around anyway in 3009. None of the people visible in the vicinity would be around either. The Marathi papers also would have all got converted into waste-paper, or would have vanished, maybe. The lovely, unkempt meadows here, spread out on the premises towards the left, they too would not remain open and free as they are now. Even if everything inside the stone building changed, there was a decent chance of the building itself staying on. Looking at its staying power till date, well, it might yet survive. But there's no telling, anyway.

It was bad, yes, whatever said and done, but then, one takes it. Some things will survive, a lot will perish, right. No newspapers of the present kind certainly, but they may very well stop coming out altogether, maybe. Which was okay, right.

– But a tree falls, and if the people do not as much as talk about a tree falling in the compound, what then?

This is NOT okay, he felt.

27 February 2010: Excerpted from an interview published in *Tehelka* –

Thirty-three-year-old Gurucharan Kisku alias Marshal walked out of the Communist Party of India (Maoist) and formed his own 150-member group in the forests of West Bengal.

'There is a difference between the demands of the adivasis and the Maoists, and this the people of India must basically understand. What we need urgently is an elevated status in our community for our language and our culture,' Kiskubhau had to say.

'The most important things for us are farms and food. We need water and canals for that. Once our stomachs are full we need education, but that through our own language. We want the same respect for our language as Bengali, Oriya and Hindi,' Kiskubhau added.

'There is no possibility of the adivasis getting justice from the present democratic process. But I have no faith in the Maoist interpretation of the Constitution either,' Kiskubhau reiterated.

Don't know what good will come out of measuring the length and width and the number of the valleys that separated Kiskubhau and Saavali Ghosh. Lovely name, Saavali, of course, but she wasn't dusky as her name suggests. She was short and fair. Went off to Kolkata after the course got over. Kemon aachho, bhaalo aachhi. Kiskubhau, chyaayla, what forests he disappeared into, don't know.

Saavali was never seen fighting with anybody. Smiled perpetually. Dressed in various kinds of clothes. Possessed seven-eight purses, likely. Wasn't tall, so wore heeled sandals. Talked a lot on the mobile.

There were many such people.

Uday was in the room. Afraid of the Marathi language politics played by a bunch of idiots, he wouldn't venture out of the room much.

Getting shop signboards done in the Devanagari script isn't going to do any good to the Marathi language, wrote Dasnurkar in an article. In a Marathi newspaper. Readers would have read. Non-readers wouldn't have read.

What, out of this, will survive in 3009?

Ten

He met Ramchandra Parab after quite a few months, in December 2009. They sat in the open canteen, drinking tea. It was cold. A little crowded. Ramchandra was tall. Painfully thin. Wasn't keeping well. Looked so much thinner because of his height. Not that there was any reason, but things were just drifting along. Ramchandra didn't come from a poor family, but not from a rich family either. The girl in the tight, white T-shirt that walked past Ramchandra looked nice.

Ramchandra smiled. Ramchandra's eyes had really sunk in. He had taken admission in Defence and Strategy Studies, not Library Science. He had lied earlier, and just for the heck of it. It was after so many months that he had come out with the truth. It's all right, really. But Ramchandra had become thin.

❖

Uday had developed a paunch, sitting in the room. 'Will have to do something,' he said.

'Do what?' He.

'Arey, these Bengalis had brought in girls yesterday.'

'That they have done plenty of times before.' He.

The Bengalis were mostly not in their room. But when they occasionally were, a girl would often be with them. Stretched out comfortably on the bed. Amazing that he should not have known for so long. It happens sometimes, though.

But Uday was putting on weight.

'The same bloody stuff, day after day. What the hell are we doing with our life?' said Mahesh Kadam. He did the district stuff with a lot of application, but would get tired once in a while. 'So bloody meaningless,' he would say. 'Don't get opportunities, won't get them either.'

Then he would sit at his computer, browsing through social media profiles of TV anchors. If he spotted a pretty girl, he'd send a friends request. 'Feels nice looking at such faces, what other use otherwise,' he would say.

The cardboard man's clothes had changed. His new dress was an unclean shirt and unclean, loose pajamas. Four-five pieces of cardboard in the left hand, and a cup in the right one, he was having tea at Tilak Road. He had had a haircut and a shave lately. Small white cup in his rough hand, he finished off the tea in three gulps. The same penetrating eyes. The wrinkles on the face thick as ever. But the old man had lost weight. He wasn't just looking thin because of the haircut and the shave, he really had become thinner.

The paper-selling woman at Tilak Road had begun to thin out too, due to cold. She continued to fade out, to the point of disappearing altogether.

'The Taj Mahal, however, is really the Tejo Mahal!' Stuff like this went on in the passionate discussion sessions Ramakant and Vrushali got involved in in the department canteen. One of these discussion-maniacs once let out that he was reading Samaveda. Another announced he was reading the Qur'an.

When Siddhesh and he overheard this, they both laughed like mad.

Lala, however, was making tea.

Patch
    Patch
    Patch
    Everything in patches.
    The doctor then told him,
    'Sar salaamat, pagdi pachaas.' (Care for the head, headgears are aplenty.)
    'Could be an ulcer. There's some intestinal bleeding. Eat and drink well, re. Don't eat sour stuff. No oranges, no sweet-lime. No oily stuff. Bananas are okay. Moong-khichdi. In small helpings. Two of the pink ones before going to bed. White ones thrice a day. Liquid thrice. What, have you got yourself a good girlfriend or not? If nothing else, success, at

least, is in your hands, right?' the doctor said with a smile.

He smiled.

The doctor was a good man.

'Come on Monday, if you feel like it.'

Just seventy rupees, including the pills.

The doctor's dispensary was near the Khajina Vihir crossing. From there he set off on Tilak Road. The newspaper woman was preparing to wind up. It was ten-thirty. Unsold copies. Her little daughter had come over to help. It was still cold. The sunshine was white. The paper-woman was close to fading away. Bare skeleton now. But she was hanging on, that she was. Laughed through her misaligned teeth. Gave her two rupees and bought a paper. Her hands were wrinkled.

Wound up and left with the girl somewhere behind there. This was how it was in January 2009.

There's an old wooden fish-tank shop where the paper-woman sits. Will open in a little while. In front, next to the post-office is the regular usal-pao man. Gram sprouts and bread. But he shouldn't be eating that so early. Further up, to the right, is the Badshaahi restaurant. Shouldn't be eating there either. Some construction under way on the right. White and red vertical stripes on tin sheets. An old woman on the footpath in front, selling newspapers. A general store next to her. An Amrut-tulya next. A baldie in rags was smoking away happily in the cramped corner. Paan-kiosk. A saloon next. Sports shop, closed. Just a building next. Wafers guy. That, by no means, chyaayla. A boy was frying potato wafers in the pan. Fumes and smell together. Crossed the road to distance himself. Ambika Amrut-tulya again to his left. The old cardboard man was there, as always, having tea.

He went in and sat down. Inside was a friend-cum-reporter named Ramesh Adhav, and another person.

'Hey, how are you? Earlier I did crime, now doing culture,' said white-shod Ramesh. Has been in journalism for five-odd years. 'Getting married. Invitation coming. Make sure you come, okay?'

He took the first sip of tea. The old man moved away with his cardboards.

The tea was terrific.

'No bomb blast in Pune, pal,' Ramesh was telling the other man. 'Hey look at that...' said Ramesh, as a fleshy girl in a sleeveless top and high heels approached the tea shop. With her was a tall boy carrying a leather bag. They ordered two cups of tea.

'Lost their way here, have they?' Ramesh. 'Pune is different. It's their strategy centre. There won't be any blast here,' resumed Ramesh, returning to his conversation with the man, divulging details he had gathered from a Malusare report.

He finished his tea. Money. Three into three nine. They still sold tea here for three rupees. Even if it was five elsewhere.

'Hey Sheyt, don't take money from him. No pal, he won't take money from you.' Ramesh.

Sheyt does not know Ramesh, knows him, so took the money.

'See you then.' Ramesh.

He stepped out. Next door was a publisher in a wooden shop, with a board that read: 'All words of the dictionary beautified here.'

❖

Ramesh Adhav won't be there in 3009. But whoever replaces him will surely not be a newsperson. Or, if he is, they'll all be newspersons. What news and what rumour? If it is only a matter of propagating, why is Malusare or Ramesh or anybody else needed? All can participate in it. Mobile and – while it is crawling now, it will be up and running some day or the other – the internet. All these together. Only, whatever the difference between news and rumour now, the difference by then will truly be even more confounding, chyaayla.

This confusion in his head stopped for some time, because a young girl sitting on the ledge beyond this bus-stop in the middle – there, right behind – was playing a song at full volume on her mobile – *Khoya khoya chaand, khulaa aasmaan, aankhon mein saari raat* –

– The possibility of this happening earlier than 3009 is quite strong. And then there will be 4009 after 3009. What does one do of that? Or 2050 arrives right round the bend, what do you do with it?

– Meanwhile, it's the Alka Talkies square. He felt then that he was going to vomit. A small passage beside this temple. Vomited. Vomited. Put some earth on it. Water. In there and in the eyes. He went in there and washed his face. Felt better. Felt lighter. For ten odd minutes, everything had just crashed.

As he went past Lakdi Pul, he saw the old cardboard man in front. How did he come back here this way? Whoever replaces him in 3009 will not be able to sit like he does, solving crossword puzzles in newspapers. All right, but he would certainly be able to sit somewhere.

Burqa-clad women seated at the parapet outside the masjid at the square. Karve Road to the left. He kept walking straight ahead. Hotter now. Towards the department. 11 o'clock.

2010
Eight dead in Pune bomb blast

Pune, 13 October: Eight persons, including a foreign national, are reported to have died in a bomb explosion that took place this evening at German Bakery near the world-renowned Osho ashram at Koregaon Park. About 50 persons have been injured, 14 of whom are said to be in a critical state. The police suspect a connection between this explosion and the extremists' attack in Mumbai and in other international cities.

The anti-terrorist squad, senior city police officials, and the fire brigade officials reached the site on receiving the news of the blast. The explosion was caused by setting off a highly destructive integrated explosive device (IED), according to information provided by officials of the Intelligence department. The explosion was loud enough to be heard across a distance of two kilometres. Body parts of the victims were seen scattered all across the street in front of the bakery. The site of the disaster presented a blood-curdling picture.

News of the explosion that occurred between 7:00 and 7:30 p.m. in the Koregaon area, spread within minutes across the city, causing deep anxiety everywhere. Newspaper offices were flooded with enquiries to confirm the authenticity of the occurrence. Some even asked whether it was a repeat of the Mumbai 26/11 catastrophe.

Eleven

It wasn't like this before,' said Tambe. Karle and he smiled. 'Aho Tambe Saheb, the past is never like today,' said Mahesh.

Having reached the end of his tether rewriting every single copy of a certain reporter's copies day in and day out, and with retirement approaching, Tambe, true to pattern, had become strongly convinced that things were different before. He would talk about the reporter everywhere, but never about the editor.

But the proofreader and the operator would talk about the editor. 'It isn't like the good old days. The editor carried such authority then,' a white-haired proofreader would say. Had crossed 60, but hadn't retired yet. 'Get the girl married in a year's time and I retire the next day,' he would say.

An operator not close to retirement, thirteen years with the paper, would say, 'It's gone. Nothing left.'

What's been?

What's seen?
What remains?
What sustains?
What ingrains?

Chuck all that, Karle said. 'Let's quaff tea instead of listening to laments.'

Karle – Mahesh – he left for tea.

Tea tea tea –

What good this sitting be?
Let's up and off for tea.
Peep in the cup – y'know –
For aught a fly or so.
' *And if a fly you see,*
Oh, well, just down the tea.

The tea sometimes gets to Karle's head, and when he gets into the mood, there's no holding him back. Mahesh and he laugh.

Not of those who ever cry, and not of those who ever laugh, the three-legged dog sat by the tree trunk, yawning in the March heat of 2009. The free-floating litter of tiny yellow leaves, a black grill next to the tree, two big benches behind it, electric meter in the room inside. Outside, a cement platform around the tree trunk. The dog sat there and yawned, the sun dappling his back. Yawned, brought his head down, and sat staring into nothingness.

1009–2009–3009–4009, the dog doesn't keep count. Doesn't count, so doesn't arrive at approximations. But that's fine. Finally, the choice is his. We have the choice too.

Was that why he started considering himself as useless? I don't know. But when the dog yawned, he had begun considering himself useless. Long before that, really.

The sun on the wall. Him sitting on the steps.

He was completely exhausted, really. The sun, not much bother about that. It's the same every year. But on his way here stopped to eat poha at the Deccan, and threw it all up when he reached the department. He shouldn't have eaten the poha, of course; but he did, and he threw it up. Then felt like all was over, so came and sat on the steps. The head completely numb.

Siddhesh came and sat on the steps, in front of him.

Let's start a collective blog.

Let's talk about things that'll survive till 2050, if not till 3009. Small is beautiful.

Tall is beautiful. 'Should we go and eat something, instead?' Siddhesh said. He'd got himself a job with an English newspaper towards the end of the course.

Called for two daal-rice thalis at the hotel in front of the department campus.

Arey, we could identify the common points among newspapers ranging from *Navaa Kaal* to *New York Times*.

From the perspective of the reader.

It may actually help us use the internet in a more sensible way, locally.

The first mouthful of the rice, and he felt he wasn't altogether useless. The food went down the gullet, and he felt: Okay, if it's useless, it's useless, so be it. As he tucked into his meal of rice with fried paapad, he began to feel that everything else is useless too. And if he alone is useless, well, so be fucking it. Useless? Okay then, useless, tichya aayla. Polished off all the rice.

Next, called for buttermilk.

It was the summer month of March 2009.

He felt better, uselessness and all.

It was not because he felt better, however, uselessness notwithstanding, but because it was a bit of a daily thing, that he went and sat on Lakdi Pul. Balasaheb sat eyeing the books. Sudhakar was eyeing the road. His man in rags was pulling at a beedi. Past 6 o'clock. The wind was dry.

Balasaheb, sitting there fingering a book, suddenly felt dizzy. The book slipped out of his hand and he toppled backwards, but because of that hump on his back, rolled to the right. He, along with Sudhakar and five-six passers-by, immediately reached his side. Couldn't be laid flat on the back because of the hump. Just didn't strike anybody at the beginning, the hump. One was trying to bring his legs down and getting quite perplexed that it refused. The head too stayed suspended midair. Then they realized that the hump was getting in the way. Slipped the hump in the cavity of the bench and made him sit there with some support. Meanwhile, somebody brought him water. Balasaheb drank the water. Someone wetted a handkerchief and mopped his face. Finally, he appeared to have returned to some kind of normalcy. Sat up without support. People dispersed.

What could have happened to Balasaheb? Age, of course. Lived across there beyond on Karve Road. Walked over here to Lakdi Pul every day in the evening and sat down. So much time killed. Reads a newspaper when he feels like it once in a while. He was a reader once.

Balasaheb recovered his poise. A little saliva was at the point of dripping out; he wiped that off with his handkerchief. Then, as he slowly recovered orientation, got up, hobbled across the square, and disappeared.

He sat on the ledge.

The fine-bosomed, round-buttocked, pink-dressed girl crossed the road with a tall boy with a black backpack, and walked towards Lakdi Pul. The tall boy nicely had his arm round her waist. Pink dupatta approaching from the left. The two-three book-browsers looked at them and smiled. The girl and the boy were smiling. Moved on towards the left.

He sat on the ledge.

Sudhakar selling books.

Man in rags pulling at a beedi.

Darkening. Clouds clouds clouds swirl swirl swirl.

A friend of his approached his spot, from the right, looking flustered. Was moving to the left when he saw him and came and sat by him on the ledge. And he started giving information on an insurance policy.

'Look it's all up to you. Put a hundred every month, na, it'll do.' Friend.

Friend pulled a laptop out of a bag and gave him information on three policies.

'Look, this one. For you, na, this you take.'

He believed the friend's work was awfully important. But

he didn't feel like insuring his life, not then at least. So he told his friend he'd think about it after six months. The friend instantly froze the topic.

'How's everything else?' Friend.

'Come let's have tea.' He.

'Come to the university some time?' The friend lives in the University hostel, as a parasite. 'Got yourself a girl, or no?'

They went from the bridge to Alka Talkies square because the friend had to go towards Tilak Road. The pink girl was having lovely, lovely tea at Regal. Friend and he moved on to a lane on the left.

'Two teas.'

There was a poster on a wall by the road.

Hon'ble Youth Leader Vikram Wagh alias Viva.

Good wishes on his 34th birthday.

A list of the well-wishers below. Roses stuck on the poster.

He asked his friend what Hon'ble could mean.

The friend said, 'Something somewhere honourable, maybe.'

'Could be a ho'n-bill, horny bill. The bird could be a maadarchod bird!' he said.

He and friend laughed on account of the poster that day.

Moving further on for his work at the next square, the friend said, 'You keep getting the policy messages, na? Come to university some time.'

Crowd on Tilak Road, including him.

Walking in a daze, when he turned into a lane just before the square after the square after the square, it had started turning dark. A hunch-backed man with a box kind of cart was making matki-bhel. He asked for 15 rupees of bhel – parcelled for takeaway. The man put fistfuls of stuff in a steel plate and swiftly mixed it up. A man at the paan shop there was smoking a cigarette. As he walked away with the parcelled bhel he noticed an extremely old woman, almost bent double, hobbling across the street with the help of a walking stick.

As the old woman crossed the road, the headlight of a motorcycle hit him in the eyes, pierced into his head.

Considering that he was keeping to the side of the road, there was no reason for the motorbike to get in front of him. It did, however, brakes screeching, headlight blinding. The motorbike man was looking to squeeze past him when he deliberately stepped in the way. If a person can't walk along the side of the road without being dashed into, it's too much. The motorbike guy flared up. Turned his bike to the other side, but he was again in the way.

'Hey bhadvya, step aside.'

He got a big kick. But before he could get a bigger kick, the motorbike man called him bhadvya and scooted away.

He had lost it for a while.

He turned into the right lane for going to his room. The lane was nice and dark, the yellow street light shining at the turn. The praajakta flowers of the morning lay scattered under the lamp-post. Before he reached the building, a stone drunk man came swaying along from the other side, the mobile in his pocket playing *Khoya khoya chaand*…

Face to face.

He shifted to the right, the drunk was to the right.

Aankhon mein saaree raat jaayegi…

He shifted left, and the drunk was right there on the left, flailing both arms.

Taare chale . . . nazaare chale . . .

Taare chale, nazaare chale, sang sang mere voh saare chale . . .

He planted himself in the middle, and the drunk got in the middle too, shifting left and right.

He hadn't consumed. The drunk had.

The ageing drunk smiled, so he too smiled.

Finally, when the drunk advanced, he moved to one side. The path was clear. He got into the building, unlocked the room, placed the bhel parcel on the table and sat on the bed.

Stories unlimited. People unlimited. Outside the room, the world, and inside, empty.

He opened up the parcel and began to eat. His eyes were burning. He had finished half the bhel when Uday walked in and asked, 'Arey, you know how to download an entire movie?'

He offered Uday some bhel but he declined. Instead of going straight for a meal, he had pointlessly brought bhel, and since he had brought it, he was eating it.

He then showed Uday how to download a movie. He also told him about Pirate Bay and stuff that some third person had told him about. Search as much as you want. Up to a level, the entire world was inside the room.

It was the summer of 2009 then and the time was well past midnight; he got into the room and lay on his bed. The window was open, in case there was a breeze. The fan was on. Years of dust on the fan. A black book on the table, 167 pages. A pale yellow vertical rectangle in the middle of the cover page, with a picture of an insect inside it. A fat, bed bug-like insect. A photograph inside of the melancholic face of a man with protruding ears. Melancholy pervaded the entire book. The man had very clear eyes.

This beautiful melancholy was present in the department library too at four-fifteen in the evening. The subject matter of this man from the room was of a hundred years ago, straight, and it lived on. The department building was a hundred years old. The man in the photograph was the writer of the 167 pages of text in the book. There is a door in the rear corner of the other classroom, permanently closed. Locked from the inside for good. Lots of cobwebs there, lots of dust, the thick wall slightly weather-beaten. The last two-three benches hardly ever used. The melancholic man could sit there. The evening rays filter in through the misty panes of the ancient doors and spread into the corner. The three-legged dog comes over sometimes to sit peaceably, in that corner. The dog will die, he will die, the building will crumble, but that man's text has spread everywhere, in books, on the internet, wide, wide, really wide. On the stone walls of the department, on the stone pathways under the banyan tree in the university, on streets, on windows.

All this frigging sentimentalism! Aaicha ghoda. Open the doors. Open the doors!

Twelve

Don't know when he started considering himself useless. Which was okay. But when did I feel a real jolt? When he realized that he felt like killing himself. This was a horrible mistake. And he knew this too. Meaning, he even felt that feeling like he wanted to die could well be the biggest uselessness of all. But then he also felt that there was a point in feeling like killing oneself, but no point in killing oneself. And quite unnecessarily, he surfed the net for answers. Are there ways of killing oneself painlessly? Or, what's wrong with only feeling like it? And while looking around for stuff of this kind he even went on to read about digital death and all that too. Honestly speaking, he knew very well that there was no point in dying. But what could he do if he felt like it? If he felt like it, well, he felt like it. Nothing else to it.

That was why then he started eating good rice thalis for both meals. 'Sar salaamat toh pagdi pachaas.' But his head ached, nevertheless, and he went on feeling like dying. He was in the middle of the market. He was walking from Mirza Ghalib Square to further past the roughed up, messed up square. Two tomatoes lay utterly squashed near a wicker basket. Garlic skin everywhere. Dark arms covered with bangles. Old woman with big red kunku sat silent. A big vehicle blocking the path. Red building. Masjid. He walked past all this and entered Bhawani Peth beyond the Ramoshi Gate Police Station and felt so awfully, completely exhausted that oh! He felt like just lying down flat somewhere. But how could he just go and lie down on his own in the middle of the road? He was completely drained. Bhawani Temple on the left, puffed rice shop on the right. Long, rusted tin sheets on the left, houses upon houses on the right. Building up there on the left, kids playing cricket on the right. Deep, dark alley on the left, open space on the right. He crossed an old motor stand, bicycle shops, a lane. On the left, there was a decent enough place to sit.

He sat. It was a small parapet. The market had been left far behind. Parsee houses from here on. A blank faced beautiful woman here with a pallu on her head selling chickoos and bananas. Wind on top stirred up the leaves on the trees. Wind below kicked up the dust on the road. Wind in the centre shook up the sunshine. He sat lightly on the parapet. Felt bored. He shut his eyes upon sitting down. Tipped his head back. The sun shone on his face. He felt better. Much better. Calm. Head felt light. He sensed the breeze. He dozed off.

He heard something, don't know what, but it woke him up. Sweat had gathered on his forehead. Legs were aching because they had been hanging idle; he realized that properly upon waking up. Half an hour had gone by. Beyond was an almond tree. Its big leaves scattered on the ground below. He got up and walked ten-fifteen steps and his legs got back their sensation. The head was heavy, but under control. Then he noticed the big, upright ice-cool Neera kiosk. He asked whoever was inside for a glass. Gave five rupees. Neera is a health-giving cold drink. Neera settles the bile. Government Recognized Neera Centre.

He turned ice-cool. One more. Five rupees.

He became cooler still.

His forehead felt nice. His head felt nice. Light. There was the sun. There was the wind. There was he.

He didn't walk on further and he just didn't turn right. Just didn't go to office. Switched off the mobile and turned left towards Lakshmi Road. Back again. He crossed the white masjid at Raviwar Peth. Then he came to the first Amrut-tulya of Pune – Arya Amrut-tulya. Came to vehicles, people, dust. Crossed bicycles, hand-carts, grills, shops. Crossed old buildings, crossed new buildings. Crossed kulfi-man. Crossed women. Crossed post office. Crossed squares. Big temples.

What was the time? Who cared?

What was the day? Who cared?

What was the year? Who cared?

When he reached Lakshmi Road, with its sophisticated shops, he began walking faster. And on the way he met a friend.

Stop.

Had no connection with journalism. Did not even read newspapers, this friend. Said, 'Come, let's have tea.'

'How come here?'

The friend had to buy a belt, so they got that out of the way.

On the bike of that friend down the one-way, and straight to the Alka Talkies square.

'There's place here to sit.'

Sat royally at Regal.

He realized how tired he was only upon sitting down.

Six-footer friend, strong built. Had his own gym on Soos Road. Big money. Had been his friend for the last four-five years. Keeps changing the style of his moustache and beard all the time.

'Take as many girls around as I can manage,' the friend said.

He smiled. The tea arrived.

'What do I say, pal, can't land a girl.' Friend.

He smiled. The first sip down the throat.

'Your media guys are big-time fuckers, are they?' Friend.

There was some kind of news about the corporator of the area who lived near the friend's house being a big nature lover, planting fifty-thousand saplings, getting a positive response from the locals on account of his efforts of converting his constituency into a green zone.

'Oh, that bastard would be uprooting fifty trees every day. He's a builder, he is.' Friend.

He was getting tired, but to the best of his ability, he tried to explain to the friend how things work. Newspapers indulge in all kinds of talk, good and bad, as much as people do. And in comparison to the bogusness elsewhere, a trivial news item on a trivial corporator doesn't count for anything. He tried to tell this to the friend with as much competence as he possessed.

'He had come to our area once, before he became

corporator. The boys gave the bastard such a licking!' The friend had a personal enmity. 'Tell me if you want somebody licked,' said the friend.

Tea over.

They stepped out. The road there. The vehicles there. The clocks there. Alongside, the evening coming in. It was past four-thirty.

At five he was sitting in the department canteen, drinking tea. The sunlight had turned yellow. It then suddenly turned ochre. Wind broke out. Looked like it would rain. Debris of leaves on the open space in front. Dark, green, cloud-soaked trees on top. Dark trunks in the middle. The three-legged dog sat to a side in the canteen. Someone had thrown him some Parle biscuits. Looked like he had eaten some, but two and a half of them still lay there in front, and as always, he lay there on the ground, lost in some reverie. Closed his eyes for a while, opened them when a passerby stooped and patted his head, and back to the quiet reverie. At the narrow white-tiled drain channel there, the tap flowed as Kishor washed the tea glasses in a big basin.

There were not many people in the canteen. There on the other side sat a tall, heavyset person with a not-so tall not-so heavyset person. A little away from them sat a bespectacled boy in a tucked-in white shirt, his hair oiled and parted on one side. In front of him, her knees scraping his, sat a dusky girl in a pink churidaar and a longish ash and pink body-hugging kameez. The churidaar showed the leafy curves of her calves. The ash and pink kameez had net-like material at the lower end and on the bodice. The contours of her breast were nicely and clearly evident. She wore a watch with a thin, brown strap on the right wrist and a gold bangle on the left one. Complexion dusky, leaning towards dark. Lips dark. Wore nothing on her ears, a gold chain round her neck. Hair left open. As she sipped her tea, the steam suffused her face every now and then.

The ochre light turned red, then vanished. It was 6 o'clock.

Someone passing by outside the canteen waved at him, he waved back.

He paid for the tea and left the canteen. A little while at the stone wall on the left. He was on the verge of turning right and leaving when he noticed Dasnurkar sitting on the wooden bench in the thick-pillared corridor on the left, looking very downcast. With his full-sleeved grey-striped shirt tucked into grey trousers, thinning hair, and lean frame Dasnurkar sat on the bench, looking downwards. Legs as if falling to one side, arms locked into one another, Dasnurkar sat there looking unblinkingly at some spot near his feet. Dasnurkar looking so listless was a strange sight. The bench was laid out along the stone wall, and Dasnurkar sat at one end. Absolutely still. Suddenly, the wind picked up and the trees shed heaps of leaves. Small, yellow, green leaves came raining down. The strange cloud cover had given the normally ashen-black earth a pale reddish hue. Dasnurkar wore black chappals. Looked very much at one with the entire department ambience, completely blending in. Stone walls, wooden doors and windows, grimy panes, two classrooms, two or three cabins tucked away in this corner or that, wooden partitions, the books in the library shelves reaching their grave, books newly arrived, the silent volumes of encyclopedias, layers of cobwebs, heaps of old newspaper, MA dissertations, PhD theses – and Dasnurkar. Looking like he had sunk real low. Didn't look up even when the wind started blowing. Looked up finally when he heard his name. Pupils moving left to right to left without looking straight up. He asked Dasnurkar what had happened. Dasnurkar stood up, lowered his mane and just walked away without even a wave of his hand. The palms of the hands alone were turned back.

Distraught Dasnurkar walked past the thick, round, stone pillars of the arched corridor. At the end of the corridor can be seen the thick trunk of a huge tree on the right, and a small hedge on the left. He turned there and headed for the gate, and out of the gate to the left. Head bowed.

He was back again on Lakdi Pul. Sudhakar selling books. Balasaheb does not come these days. Could well have passed away. The other group of oldies comes. He of course was there. Plenty of others were there too.

His mobile was still switched off. It was past seven. He switched the mobile on later. So many had their mobiles on. Well, all right.

He was feeling quite pooped out. Sitting on the ledge. The light faded away. The big white lamp above lit up. Something flashed near the International Book Depot. There were the headlights. There was the burning end of the beedi Sudhakar's helper in rags was smoking. There were people. Moving around.

There was dust. There was the dark peepal tree behind.

He felt squeezed.

Pressed.

Got up.

Turned left again. A road passed below the bridge. The black river passed. A strip of green grass passed. A gust of wind came along. Black sky overhead. Wind from here, from there. From here, from there.

He was back at the Alka Talkies square.

Vehicles after vehicles – lights after lights – round after round – line after line.

Blinking signals – insignificant people – trivial he.

The entire square from here to there, from there to here.

He, however, reached Tilak Road. It was dark. The big red boxes of the electric people. He was just walking down the footpath when he felt a knock on the back of his head and a rip on his right arm. The knock made him collapse on one side of the footpath. A truck had hit him as it crossed him, its heavy chain on the rear grazing him on the head and a jutting-out edge of the iron sheet ripping his sleeve and leaving a cut on his upper arm.

Nobody quite understood what happened. By the time he realized something the paan-kiosk man there and two or three others had run up to him.

He felt like it was all over for him.

Then realized it wasn't all over.

When he sat at the table next to the paan-kiosk, he sensed a little pain behind the right ear. Blood on the right upper arm. Two or three people around. He gave them a handkerchief. One tied it round the arm. It burned. The water arrived. He drank some, splashed some on his face.

The pain behind the ear was not too bad. The pain on the upper arm was. They fetched some turmeric from a shop, removed the handkerchief, applied it on the wound and tied the handkerchief back. It burned again.

He was now registering everything quite nicely. The paan-guy and the others asked him whether he felt all right. He said yes. Sat for a little while. When he felt better he informed them and left.

The street was ticking, the vehicles were ticking, people were ticking.

He was lying very still in the cot in his room. Fan on. Lights off. Windows open. He just lay on the cot. Very tired. Right arm was really throbbing. There was a sensation behind the right ear, but it wasn't paining much. There was a bottle of water below the cot. He drank a little bit of the water and stayed still. The mobile beeped some message or something, so he looked it up. Switched on the radio. The darkness was there. He was there. The table was there. There was a black book on the table. 292 pages. The flip side was purple. The cover page was black, with the face of a man on it. Greyish hair brushed back, moustache, prominent, thick, black-stemmed spectacles. The collar showed too. The photograph was of the author of the book. He began writing sometime in the mid-1950s and died in 1999, yet the subject matter of his book was alive in 2009. Could be alive in 3009 too. The author's piercing eyes were clearly visible through the spectacles.

He adjusted the volume of the radio such that the songs would be clear and the chatter in the interim not so much.

The songs playing on the one side. The arm throbbing on the other. The night was deepening bit by bit. The RJs go a bit quiet at night, so there was less chatter on the radio. Outside the window, a beautiful, quiet, big yellow light near the neighbouring building. His head had quieted on its own. He recalled now the coming of the truck. He recalled falling to the side. He recalled thinking that all was over. As he lay there, recalling the incident, sleep began to overpower him. Didn't know what song the radio was playing, but went into peaceful slumber.

Tere mere sapne ab ek – he heard, as he woke up. Didn't know what the time was. The author of the book said, 'Never seen another actor like Waheeda.' He felt great. *Rang hain – jahaan bhi le jaayein raahein* – the song from the movie *Guide* playing. The author pulled out a photograph of Waheeda Rehman from his wallet. 'People who cared for Waheeda felt happy when she got married. I felt happy too. But it pricks the heart too,' laughed the author of the book. He was now wide awake. *Tere mere sapne ab ek rang hain* – the song was still playing. The author of the book didn't stir. But the contents of the book, its paragraphs and chapters, they were floating around him. 'Waheeda's film, *Teesri Kasam*, was playing the other day on the television, and all her fans, including Raj Kapoor, saw an image that churned up a person's insides. Her beauty just hypnotized the senses. And we too, finally, the way Raj Kapoor gets all worked up na, we too had got all unhinged kind of, thinking of her. Didn't abandon the world either, of course, that's true. But then I felt that I should swear never again to see Waheeda's movies that so rake up the memories and open up old wounds.'

Time, age, day, night – all vanished. Waheeda Rehman turned old. Danced a slow dance to the song *Sasuraal genda phool*. This movie from early 2009 also brought back memories of the author. Fifty-sixty years here and there, nothing special about that. All the stuff about Hindi pictures, whatever there is, well, there is. A writer who could go beyond that and talk – that rattled him.

A movie of 1965. 2009. 3009.

Buildings, structures, trees, people kept coming and moving.

The melancholic author mentioned earlier looked inside with clear eyes, and now this thick-framed-spectacled author looked outside with clear eyes. The same, exactly.

Thirteen

Meanwhile, plenty happened.

Tambe was dismissed. He was due to retire anyway, so not much damage caused. Not to him, not to others.

The proofreader delaying retirement for his daughter's marriage was dismissed.

Another shortish proofreader who came to work on a battered M80 was dismissed.

There was this operator built like a wrestler – he was dismissed. Tall and hefty, he would sit in a corner and type away. Brought a rather small tiffin-box, compared to his size. Sat and ate alone somewhere too.

One tiny operator, who was forever busy making new email IDs for himself – he was dismissed too. He would forget his password, so he jotted it down somewhere. But he would lose that too and have to open a new email account.

A simple, loud-speaking operator was dismissed.

A young sub-editor who gave too much lip to the editor

was dismissed.

Chief sub-editor Jairam Jadhav (age 49) passed away. Organic farming was his area of special interest. He had been in journalism for twenty years. He was renowned for being a journalist who physically toiled in the farm as well. He had received the Krushi Mitr Award from the State Government the previous year. He is survived by his wife, a daughter, and a son. Single column item with photograph for all editions imperative.

Mahesh Kadam got himself a slightly better-paying job in a slightly smaller newspaper, so he left.

Ranade, Bhosale and Malusare were promoted. A mid-level editor retired.

The Pune supplement was whittled down from six to four pages. Went to pieces. Lots of news items had to be dropped.

'Ours is a boat sinking under the weight of just a few people who have become heavier than they need be, saala,' said Karle while having tea.

Tea increases bile, the doctor had said, so he had cut down on his tea anyway. He was thus sitting in the canteen, cutting down on his tea, when it began to rain. The clouds gathered all of a sudden, the wind picked up, and it began to descend, drop, drop, drop. The few people who were there in the canteen took shelter under the tin-roof. Ramakant-Vrushali and he were sitting on three chairs. The rain started pouring heavily. A streamlet trickled out from under a wooden plank on the left and began collecting along the stone near his legs. The streamlet swelled by degrees. Sayli and Jayesh came and sat on the other side. Slightly wet, hair on face, water on arms and nape, smiling teeth, wrinkles by the eyes. Drops had formed on the barbed wires atop the stone ledge there. Patter patter patter. The boy named Ramakant was talking about how there is politics everywhere and what a smart person a journalist named Malusare is, and the girl named Vrushali was listening to him. He was too. A few drops visible on the back. The wall stones got wet. Rain on the panes too. It fell a drop at a time through a tiny hole in the tin roof and landed a span away from where his foot was. Kicked up a bit of earth with each drop. Patter patter patter it fell on the trees. It fell under the trees. It fell among the green leaves. It fell upon the dry, black leaves. Wet hair loosened and gathered up again. Rain inside the panes. In the library, on the cuddapah, on the shingles, down the shingles. Rain. On the dusky mane in front, on the ears, rain. In the eyes, on the lids, rain.

It was raining in Pune. The rest of the time spent on the slushy streets. Now, he was in his room. He could see the rain outside the window. Lots of dust had settled on this side of the window. The drops caused dust stains in the beginning. Then it all got washed clean. He could see the rain on the white wall of the building there. He sat relaxed on a chair. Asked him how he felt. Nice, he said. Rain stopped. A flock of pigeons on the parapet of the white walls of the building there.

Outside, it all looked sharp, sharp blue. The evening would be bowing out. The blue so sharp that the darkness of the room looked blue too, starkly blue, purple in patches. Out there to one side, behind there, right behind there, you could see the branches of a praajakta tree. Below it was a tin roof. A spread of don't-know-how-old praajakta leaves, black, brown, very few green. A tyre there. A tiny wooden shrine. A plastic bag, white, lay pasted there. All of it lay wet and dejected there, and the cool, blue wind wafted over it.

He had to get the wound on his right upper arm bandaged. There was no point at all in dying, he knew it well enough, really. But then he would sink so, so low out of utter exhaustion that okay, he would feel like it. Just felt like going to sleep, that's it. But the author looking inside said there's no point in dying, and the author looking out said there's point in staying alive. The same, really.

He hadn't known well enough earlier how important this business of eating was. He knew now. He saw now that food is a bloody important thing. The head went leaden and creaked, toppled over, the ears imploded, the legs gave in, that's when comprehension came. The real truck came, the truck of the dream came, and he got the picture. He bled from the mouth, he bled from the arm, and understood extra-special.

Editors will change, newspapers will start, newspapers will close down; the inner story of everything across the globe, all the politics, the we-know-it-all level of news dispatches will come, will stop coming. Over-sentimental, zero-sentimental articles will come, will stop coming. Even if knowledge dies in the information explosion, even so, information on knowledge will remain somewhere on the internet. Less – more, up – down, all of this will keep going on, and food has a big role to play here; it took him a little time to make this connection. And that's all right too, all said and done.

Municipal Corporation, Public Newspaper Library.
Sadashiv Peth, Jondhale Chowk, Pune – 30.
Newspaper: the fourth pillar of democracy!
God in Work
Contentment in God
Where there is contentment
There resides Lakshmi.
As he was reading this board on Kumthekar Road, the Pune edition of a newspaper was taking its last hiccups. Crisis of news. Big time crisis. Five proofreaders, but no matter to read. Where there is matter, no pages to lay it on. Where there are pages, nothing in hand anyway. Chief reporter has left. He had taken with him all those employees that were close to him.

The reading kind would read the Saturday/Sunday supplements. The non-readers didn't read. The rest were getting along nicely – speeches, discussions, blogs, TV, Facebook.
A newspaper company folded.
That was okay, really.
But words lost their worth,
That was not okay, really.

The old cardboard man was busy with his own rounds. The three-legged dog sat quiet, nicely busy sitting quiet. Sudhakar sold his books as he always did. The fine-bosomed round-buttocked girl and the black-backpack toting tall boy were getting along famously. Uday with gutka and his laptop, laptopping away as ever. Jayesh–Sayli, well, they were carrying on merrily too. Karle was around. Mahesh Kadam was around. The tree that fell on 20 January 2009, the trunk was still pulsating. Doesn't go till it is rooted out, literally.

The trees were there, the wind was there, the leaves were there, the buildings were there, the streets were there.

That was when Kanu Sanyal committed suicide.

Kanu Sanyal committed suicide in the summer of 2010. In a small hamlet neighbouring Naxalbari in West Bengal. One of the founding members of the Naxalite movement committed suicide. Later, within a fortnight, the Naxalites blew up 76 policemen, but that's another story. And Kanu Sanyal went and committed suicide there. Eighty-one years and bald, wore thick, framed spectacles. Whatever the similarities of thought between him and Che Guevara, there was no similarity in looks at all. The CIA guys bumped Che off in Bolivia, and here this man goes and commits suicide.

Fourteen months before Kanu Sanyal committed suicide, a movie was playing on the old TV in the wooden case in the other classroom. Lights off, curtains pulled. Sukhatme had set it on play, with the remote working. Nine odd people in the classroom.

The sounds of a city.

Construction work half done on a big, grey building. Window frames with the slab laid. Stairways naked.

A small boy is playing with a rabbit down below. A

sixteen-odd-year-old girl in a frock enters, and runs away with the rabbit. The boy runs after her. Thump thump thump thump. The boy's mother at the gate calls after him. The boy leaves his play midway.

The girl in the building. The rabbit slips out of her hands. She runs after the rabbit. Thump thump thump thump. Rabbit has vanished. The girl is running through the building. In, in, up, up.

Up there, in front, two young boys lying drunk, propped up against the wall. One dark, the other fair. The girl stops in her track, startled. The fair boy surfaces at the sound of her stopping. The darkie continues to sleep, with his saxophone lying next to him. The fair guy runs his eyes over the girl. Sets right the empty bottle at the end of his stretched out legs. The girl is still. The fair guy's eyes fixed on her. He gets up. She retracts. He advances. She runs. He sets after her. Thump thump thump up up thump thump thump.

Wall in front. The girl halts. Back against the wall. The boy is in front. He goes nearer. And nearer. The girl manages to slip away. Runs to the left and then – scream. Falls off the edge, over the half-done wall.

Falls on a cross-beam, head first. Dead. On the slab up there, the dark boy sits playing a soulful tune on his saxophone. Quiet all over.

A twenty-minute story.

Girl gone. City gone. Building gone. Saxophone.

He felt as if both the in-looking and the out-looking authors sat by the saxophone boy. Their role was the same. The news of the girl's passing away would appear in the papers the next day.

Fourteen

An empty road in the far-flung campus of Pune University. There are some spots in the university that are quite deserted.

Road. Nice and wide. Champa trees on both sides. Leaves have all shed. Empty, black trunks, black branches. Champa flowers scattered all along the tar road. White, yellowish inside. Pebbles, flowers alongside the road. Black shadows of trunks and branches entangled into one another.

He met a man there with some kind of a problem with his left leg. Soiled white kurta, grey trousers, salt-and-pepper stubble on the chin, bald. Around seventy years of age. Native of some place around Osmanabad. Came over during the famine of '71-'72, and stayed on. Lives with somebody in the university. Meals are arranged for, sleeps in the temple. He used this road for his walks.

Road. Wide. Where it ends are two culverts on either side, and barren open sun-bathed ground spread out in front.

He is sitting on the culvert. Champa flowers on the culvert too. There was no point in asking him about his job.

Asked him, what happened to this business of wanting to die?

This was the more important question.

He shrugged his arms. There was no point in staying on that topic. There was some point in feeling so, but that's about it. What more left to say? If one felt that way, one felt that way. It was a mistake. If the mistake happened, what the devil does one do? On the contrary, it was good that he felt it and went on to move beyond. Lost six kilos in the stupid racket, but okay, fine.

He is sitting on the culvert.

Asked him, what to do about this uselessness?

So he laughed. What else? Can't do a thing, he said. Don't really know why he started considering himself useless and since when. He never opened up to me on this subject, and one cannot compel anyone to talk about this kind of thing. And what's to be gained by opening up either? And that uselessness of his caused nobody any harm, did it? He was nicely and peacefully useless, and that's it.

Yeah, that's okay too. So much better than dying, this considering oneself useless.

That was why I never asked him this kind of question again. Useless, so okay, useless then. He's finished a good lunch. Now he sits peacefully on the culvert. Around four in the afternoon. The sun, the warmth, the shadows, all neatly in place. He'll go for tea in a little while. Rest is fine.

Three Contexts of a Writer

To
Sahir Ludhianvi
&
Albert Camus

First Context

One

A tiny structure on the table: seven-cornered, three-inch tall, thick glass. Nicely flat at the bottom. A hole at the top. Dry looking leaves, green and red, floating in the water trapped in the middle. Shake the piece, and the leaves drift across the seven corners. Dry, green and red leaves drifting inside the glass.

'What is it?' I asked.

'Pen-stand,' he replied.

He on that side of the table, I on this. A five-by-four table in the middle. Off-white sunmica topped, with computer, keyboard and mouse on it. I sat on a heavy wooden chair on this side of the table. An empty wooden chair next to me. The table in the middle. He sat there on the other side, stretched out peacefully, hand behind head, in a big blue chair designed for stretching out peacefully.

The ten-by-ten room is in a sturdy old stone building. It's his office. Right behind the blue chair where he sits is a small window with vertical iron bars. To the right of where he sits, that is, to my left, is a similar but bigger window. Vertical iron bars. A horizontal iron strip runs through the middle. The shutters are wood, with four square panes.

Outside the window, the branches and leaves of the oudumber tree that grows in the compound. Also visible is a small white patch of the neighbouring building. A road runs through the middle. Vehicles to and fro. More buildings on the other side of the road. A gulmohar tree in full bloom.

The first shower of the season. Wet out there, including the road. A splattering of red gulmohar on the black road with a smattering of small green leaves. Raindrops here and there.

In my hands the pen-stand that has never held a pen. Picked it up to count the leaves: how many green and how many red. Each leaf about half an inch. Seemed a good way to kill time. Couldn't manage. Asked him, 'How many green, how many red?'

He asked, 'Are there red in there?'

'Chyaayla,' I laughed.

'What? You didn't know?'

'Arey, all I know is that leaves are green,' he said.

I was nonplussed.

He: 'I really cannot distinguish when this green and red come together. I am colour-blind.'

That quite stumped me.

Wet gulmohar outside.

In his thirtieth year he got truly confused. Not to suggest that he wasn't confused earlier. But true confusion began for him when he was around thirty. Earlier, it was like this:

Once, when he was in the sixth grade, he drew a picture of the coronation ceremony of Shivaji. It was a nice little drawing book. White ducks on blue water, four of them. Green grass around, lots of it. It had a red border, the cover of the drawing book. He loved it. The sixth grade year had just begun. The usual enthusiasm of the first few days, and the rains too. He had another book that carried the picture of the coronation of Shivaji Maharaj. He didn't care for history as a subject, but this picture was impressive. He had tried his hand at sketching once in grade five, but had just messed it up. Chucked away seven efforts in a crumpled ball. But in the July of grade six, he got it right. Properly right. He had a red Nataraj pencil. A look at the sketch, and he was impressed at his efforts. Shivaji Maharaj seated on a throne up there on the right. Milling crowd in the durbar, a few lieutenants, two English officials in front, bent over. All the grandeur of the coronation scene. A riot of colours. And that was where he took wings.

The pencil sketch looked grand. Now he had to fill it with colours. So he brought over his brand-new crayon set of thirty-two colours and got to work. He looked carefully at the colours in the book and started filling them into his sketch with as much exactness as possible. Seated cross-legged on the floor, he bent over double and concentrated hard as he went on colouring his sketch to match the original. He was thrilled with himself. Showed it to the people at home. Got wows from everybody. Who's not thrilled at their own child? So that was it. One Sunday spent on the sketch.

When he reached school the next day, he showed the sketch to his bench-mate. The bench-mate laughed loudly and said, 'What mad-cap colouring have you done?' He took the drawing-book and passed it on to the kids in front. They too guffawed in scorn. They passed it on to the two on the right, who laughed too. They passed it on to the ones behind, and the book travelled forwards and backwards and rightwards and leftwards. It circulated a little more in the rear among the two girls' benches. A guy good at kabaddi showed it to a girl wearing a watch with a brown strap. She giggled into her handkerchief and went and sat in her place.

That killed him.

By mid-day break, everything had returned to normal. Not he. His bench-mate later asked him how come he had done green there, and the red was too dark here, and it had all turned green there. He heard it out. Confusion had set in. During the class before the mid-day break, he had thrust his hand inside his satchel, torn the sketch out of the drawing book, crumpled it, and let it stay in. As soon as school broke for the day, he ran down to the basement and threw the crumpled paper into the dustbin.

He set off towards his classroom on the first floor for his tiffin. He looked down as he passed the girl wearing the watch with the brown strap on the stairs. There was another girl with her. They were laughing as they came down the stairs. That jolted him. His throat tightened at the sight of the laughing girls. Why were they laughing?

He ate a gloomy tiffin that day.

Something or the other of this kind happens, and something or the other comes to mind. There was some kind of puja at his house once, so he and his cousin had set off to collect flowers. That killed him again. Collected a whole lot of tagar flowers. Little green leaves, pretty white flowers. He was particularly fond of these flowers, in fact. And that was why he headed towards that tree first. The trees were right along the embankment. Lovely trees, lots of them, one next to the other. He had a blue receptacle in his hand, nice and round and dandy. He plucked whatever flowers he could spot and put them in the receptacle. The cousin was on the other side. When he got on top of the embankment, the cousin called out, 'Hey, get that one.'

'Where?' he asked.

'Arey, there on top of the jaswand branch there!' said the cousin.

'Where?'

'Arey, right along the right hand side, see!'

Dead yet again. He just couldn't see the flower. He scanned the branch to the right. That it was not tagar was clear as daylight. He recognized the jaswand by the shape of its leaves, but its flowers he just couldn't see! Chyaayla. Then he took stock of all the shapes he could see along the right hand side, and plucked out one.

'Messed it,' said the cousin.

He didn't understand. When he put the shape into the receptacle he saw the torn reddish jaswand flower.

Boundless blue sky above.

There always are childhood stories of this kind.

In the sixth grade, at least, the girl who wore the watch with the brown strap was taller than him. This is another of those stories. The girl he had noticed on the stairs on the day of the sketch.

Another such tale from the seventh grade too. There was a bibba tree in the school compound. If its sap touches the skin, the skin breaks out into big blisters. So he had this friend in his class named Jayaraj. This Jayaraj once gathered the sap from the bibba tree and 'tattooed' the word 'Macho' on his bicep. The sap burns the skin nicely and leaves behind a 'tattoo'. So Jayaraj went and wrote 'Macho' on his bicep. He then pushed up his sleeve and showed him the tattoo. Jayaraj was a sturdily built boy, a good deal sturdier than him for sure. And now the word 'Macho' on his bicep. He went and told the other boys about it. Jayaraj then pulled up his sleeve in class and showed it to the other boys too. When the class-teacher got to know about it, she really lost it. For two days running she made him stand outside class, holding his ears with arms looping up from below his knees – the 'murga' posture. Jayaraj otherwise was not a mischievous boy. But he got into such freaky acts once in a while. Later, he went on to do some truly freaky acts and died on the road. But that was way, way later. And that was Jayaraj's story. We are with his story now.

He was good at kabaddi during his school days. If not quite the first, he was second or third on the list of the class kabaddi team. Earlier, when his height wasn't much, he enjoyed a big advantage. He wasn't easily trapped. It was during the seventh grade that he played kabaddi the most, and then, just stopped playing that very year. Because he started suffering from asthma. That is, he had to give up kabaddi because he started suffering from asthma.

It wasn't as if he felt awfully bad having to give up kabaddi. Quite the contrary, he would forever be losing his shirt buttons and tearing his shorts. And from the eighth grade onwards he got into playing volleyball, and then he quite forgot kabaddi, almost.

Volleyball, though, was grand. A big rectangle. Split into two sections by a net raised in the middle. Two teams, one on either side. The ball tossed from this side to that, that to this. No too much of running around. And there were lots of decent players too, which meant there would be lots of people on both sides. Nine-and-ten or ten-and-eleven, some such odd-even numbers. The responsibility, then would be on you only when the ball came to you.

Often they played so that nobody lost. The ball would just get knocked about from hand to hand. Not everybody liked this kind of play, though. But once in a while he played with Jayaraj or Sunil after school. That was when the ball just stayed in the air, shuttling from this side to that, from that to this, sometimes for fifteen minutes. That was fun too. He loved to serve too. Threw the ball high up in the air. This was quite unnecessary, he just got hooked on serving very high. But then that was another kind of fun.

In the eighth grade he was told he didn't have asthma, after all. But sometimes during the seventh he had been quite breathless, and the people at home had jumped to fancy conclusions. They never got around to visiting a doctor, and in all that hoopla kabaddi slipped away. The upshot of all that was that he landed up in volleyball and began liking it more than he had liked kabaddi. Exams, studies, this kind of stuff rolled along as they do with everybody else. No separate effort needed for that. His marks weren't on the real high side, but they weren't low either. Just once, when in the ninth, he got very low marks in history, but that was his worst.

Here's another one from the ninth. Not related to school.

Jayaraj asked him once, 'Want to come over to our side to play?' There was a natural playground near where Jayaraj stayed; that is, they didn't have to work at fixing that ground. Big open space with a strip of grass spread evenly across. Where there was no grass the boys had done up a pitch for playing cricket. It was great.

They rustled up two teams of nine each side. He was in Jayaraj's team and they batted first. He got a few good strokes going and made forty-four runs. Ten-over match. The team rustled up ninety-four runs. All went well till that point. The red rubber ball was great for hitting. His bowling wasn't up to much. As a result, when their turn came to field, his main job was just fielding. And Jayaraj asked him to field on a grassy patch. Gone! He knew he was done for. The ball didn't come his way during the first over, and he survived. The third ball of the second over he saw coming his way, but it disappeared when it entered the grassy patch. The bowlers and the others were yelling away, and he standing still. He first thought he should pretend to fall, but while he was thinking that, three runs had been taken. Jayaraj picked up the ball from near his feet and threw it in. Slapped him on the head and said, 'Can't you bloody see?' Fact is, he actually couldn't see the ball.

One more from the ninth grade. The arm of the girl with the brown-strapped watch had brushed against his. A thrill had run through him, an electric current.

The thing was that boys and girls didn't talk to each other, not in their school either. In the rarest of rare circumstance, a programme or a competition or something, someone would exchange a rare something some time, and that would be it. So there was never any chit-chat of any kind. This being, then, the state of affairs, he was once moving up the stairs. The brown-strapped-watch girl was coming down the stairs. And almost certainly by accident her left arm brushed against his right arm. Distinctly brushed, and he held her little finger for exactly three seconds.

One

    two

        three.

She looked up at him. What lovely tendrils on her face! The line of a very slim gold chain on her neck. He had let go of her little finger by then. What a delicate, soft finger it was too! Well, if a few words had been exchanged on the stairs, it wouldn't have created any scandal, certainly! That degree of freedom did exist. But she didn't say anything. He wouldn't have said anything either, but he did, 'Lovely watch you got there.' She smiled and moved on.

This lasted him through his tenth grade.

Twisting his own little finger, he would sit staring at her. At her brown-strapped watch. At whatever chain was visible. At the tendril and at her face. At her nape and at her feet. The uniform after the eighth grade was shalwaar-suit and dupatta for girls and trousers and half-sleeved shirt for boys. A thin gold bangle arrived on her wrist in the tenth grade. One little finger lasted him through the tenth grade.

They crossed each other on the stairs many times after that, up down, down up, but their arms never brushed again. But her look thrown in his direction would be enough for him. The look he gave her and the glance she would cast at him. It was sharp, that glance of hers. Steady black pupils. In all honesty, he got a scare a couple of times, but exactly then she would give a smile.

See, he would be looking at her all the time in class, that of course, but on the stairs too he would clearly be eyeing her. She didn't look at him often, but she did throw an occasional look at him too. The look was very cold and very hot. He felt both sensations from her glance. There were times when he would just disintegrate and lie with his head on the desk. And occasionally, she would suddenly smile and bring back memories of the little finger he had held. Her eyes were very sharp. It was all right when she was smiling. But when she was not smiling and merely cast a look at him with her clear, clear eyes, he would just get blown away.

What eyes!

He went into arts. 'Will do a PhD in Economics,' is what he would say when somebody asked, which is what he said to the people at home too. Even otherwise, if he had done science, his family would not have been able to support him for further studies. He didn't have the vaguest idea what he would do with a commerce degree. Arts, therefore, was clearly the simplest option. No point taking tension.

Only, it would mean commuting by bus. He lived in the suburbs, see, so he would take the bus to and from college. Took around twenty minutes each way. The bus would occasionally be crowded, but most of the time he would find a seat.

In the early days, it once happened that it was drizzling

a bit. The roads were a little slushy. He got into the bus and did not see any seat vacant in front on the right. Saw one on the left and took it instantly. With the drizzle getting in from the window, the left of the seat was sort of wet. He was comfortably seated. Others were comfortably seated. Two stops came, two stops went. The bus became more crowded. An old woman got in and sat next to him, on the wetter side of his seat, towards the window. He realized that a girl in a dark-red shalwaar and a light-green full-sleeved kameez was standing by his side. She was older than him. He looked down and felt a pain in his brows. Just then, the girl tapped him on the shoulder and pointed at what was written on top of the window: 'Reserved for Ladies'. In effect, she was telling him to vacate the seat for her. He suddenly felt angry. But what, after all, could he do? He was sitting there with his backpack, dressed in grey trousers and a lemon-yellow shirt. The girl was older and he was just sprouting a trace of downs on his upper lip.

She was wearing a light-green kameez and a dark-red shalwaar. He was left with no choice but to vacate the seat. As he got up, his head brushed against her chest. He was furious, but there was nothing he could do. He felt as if everyone in the bus, including all the men, were watching him. The girl got into his head…

…and into his dreams that night. She was not wearing the dark-red shalwaar. She was wearing the light-green kameez, though. There wasn't another soul in the entire bus, but she came straight up to him and said 'Get up.' And he got up. She stretched out on the seat. She was barefoot. It began to drizzle from the roof of the bus. She got wet. Round breasts.

She was staring angrily at him. Then she smiled. Went and sat on another seat, with her right leg crossed over her left one. Greenish kameez hitched up from below. He saw her fair thighs.

And he melted below the waist.

Felt like he was stretched out on a patch of green.

He began writing poetry too on reaching the eleventh grade. It's not as if he had read other people's poems or anything. He first saw crowded poetry reading gatherings only after getting into the eleventh. It was somewhere in the middle of the eleventh grade, just a little after Diwali, that poems began coming to him. It had turned quite cold and wintry. It was from that winter till the winter of his twenty-seventh year that he remained poetry-infected. So, for about nine-ten years, he wrote steadily and regularly, even if not as a routine. Why up to the winter of the twenty-seventh year? Because that was when he really derived physical pleasure from and gave physical pleasure to a woman. Comprehensively. For the very first time. But that comes later.

All this, though, began in the eleventh. Love, tears, letters, sky, arms, legs, these formed the subject matter of his poetry. They formed a group in college on the strength of their poetry, some ten-twelve of them. These developments happened right after the Diwali of that year. All doing poetry. There were just three girls in the group, and poems were many.

The tears that stream down your eyes
The misty wind when espies
The bright star, it sighs
And brightness spreads across the skies

This was among his first five poems from the eleventh grade. His group would gather every Sunday for poetry reading sessions. They were all in great form. A few others joined the group later. Everything was steeped in poetry.

The world of lectures and stuff continued on the one side. But the thing that really enveloped him was the world of poetry. There were other students in class, but they were totally outside this world.

One such outsider told him once towards the end of the twelfth grade: 'You pricks, all of you, you do poetry, right? Ever read Tukaram?'

It wasn't as if that set him on fire. But he did feel a little put off. The Tukaram flaunter was also a friend, in a way.

> *Each household doth a poet own*
> *Yet not a single dulcet tone*
> *This craze for vulgar filigree*
> *That hath no care for pedigree*
> *No point in breaking into a sweat*
> *Just make your own whate'er you get*
> *Says Tuka, yes, they surely know*
> *But willy-nilly blind they go*

That's what that friend recited to him of Tukaram. They were all speakers of Marathi. But he did feel that the friend had no business dumping unasked advice on him! Wasn't even a close friend. Just a casual acquaintance.

There was an exceptionally pretty girl in class during eleventh and twelfth. Everybody had fallen for her. She had a fancy wardrobe too. And she wore her dresses with abandon.

A Punjabi shalwaar-suit cut low at the back, another near-transparent loose-fitting white kurta, reaching up to her thighs, that she wore with black jeans, a host of other really fancy clothes.

He would eye her too, along with everyone else, but that only occasionally. Beauty of this dimension didn't fit in snugly within his lifestyle. He had five pairs of clothes. The best shirt and trousers were kept reserved for special occasions. That left four pairs, three T-shirts with trousers, and one extremely ordinary pair of shirt and trousers. Plus two more T-shirts. Besides, he travelled by bus.

However, he did float around a bit once.

The Sunday that fell after the Diwali of grade twelfth, their group had assembled as always. There were quite a few others who had arrived with some or the other person. Miss Bombshell had come too. Tight white leggings under a light-green sleeveless kameez. Oh boy, killing! And high-heeled sandals to boot!

Things were flowing along as usual in this world. Poetry reading. Hey, that's superb! Oh wow! Beeyootiful! Oh lovely! Clap clap!

The whip of your stole
Sent me soaring high
When earthwards returned
Found just a pillow nigh

When he began with the recitation, somebody clapped joyously. Somebody else said 'Hey, that's great!' He held his notebook tighter, and went on:

The sky and all its illusions
Created in me delusions
Then I took a decision
Then...
...took a decision
Looked at the skies
Snapped all ties
Time now all over lies

Thunderous ovation. Then two-three others read out their poems. Applause followed. The programme wound up in the regular fashion. There's a nice little hangout area just a little this side of college, on the inner side. There was this jackfruit tree near the parking lot, and that's where this hangout was. So, well, programme over. Some had come on bikes, they left on their bikes. Those who had walked in walked away. His bus stop was on the right as you leave. He had a friend with him at the bus stop, one of the group, waiting for another bus in another direction.

That's when Bombshell came along on her bike, halted near the stop, and called him over with a wave of her hand. Deep, round neckline her kameez had. 'Your poem was nice,' she said. Her name was Sonali. Sonali told him that his poem was nice, and she smiled. There was a gold chain around her neck too. 'Thanks,' he said.

'Next time I'll bring a stole,' she gave another smile and said.

'No no, you look nice this way.'

'So I won't look nice with a dupatta?'

'Oh you do look nice, but you look nicer without the dupatta,' his self-confidence had swelled.

She smiled again and said, 'Thanks.' He scanned her from her thighs down till below her knees.

'Drop you somewhere?' Sonali asked.

He wasn't that confident, so he said, 'No, thanks, I've got a pal with me.'

'Okay, bye then,' Sonali smiled.

He waved goodbye, went back to the bus stop, and just floated away.

Floating, floating ever so softly, he travelled home. The outline of Sonali's back as she rode away on her scooter travelled home with him.

Sonali visited him in his dreams that night. Dressed in the clothes of the afternoon, with a white dupatta added. The back was completely bare. No dupatta. He close to her knees. She sat leaning against the wall. Oh, her calves. And then, Jayaraj, with clean-shaven head, the word 'Macho' clearly visible on his arm.

He woke up with a jolt.

Chyaayla, how the devil did Jayaraj barge into the dream?

He turned his face back to the dream. With firm resolve, he began his dream about Sonali's calves. Sonali smiled. She rested her lips on his cheek. Pulled him closer. And he melted below the waist.

He was literally floored when he actually ran into Jayaraj. He was in his first year. Jayaraj suddenly materialized in front of him and simply ran into him. Jayaraj's right arm was covered with blood. He and two others went running towards the college gate and sped out. The collision had sent him sprawling. He got up and dusted his trousers. Just didn't understand what was going on. All he registered was Jayaraj.

There were some poster-sticking groups in college. Groups with names like Prestige Group, Indian Group, Rebel Group, Jana-Gana-Mana Group, and such like. A new group would keep sprouting occasionally. Most of the time the posters dealt with programmes like fashion show, ball dance, Bhagat Singh's anniversary, and stuff. Very occasionally there would be posters protesting against petrol price hike or some such issue. That again was another world. It was in this other world that differences sprang up between two groups. So one group called over boys from outside, and Jayaraj was among them. They smashed a tubelight on a boy's head. Created a big ruckus. For a full week policemen were posted at the college gates. The boy who'd had the tubelight smashed on his head returned after a fortnight, and got back to strutting around the college, now sporting a white bandage, quite in the style of a Hindi film hero.

'Hindi picture' it was, all right. When Jayaraj sent him sprawling on the ground, that was out and out Hindi picture stuff played out at his expense.

By the time the boys arrived, yelling 'Abey maadarchod, stop,' Jayaraj and his two companions had cleared out of the gate.

However, sitting through a Hindi picture was a sore punishment for him. It was worse if it was the romantic kind. All that colour really confused him. The head would start aching at a particular spot. Their poetry-reading group once went for some such kind of a movie, god knows which one. To his left was a friend from the group. To his right was a female friend. There were some seven-eight of them altogether. From the very start, his right knee and right upper arm were brushing against the girl's left knee and upper arm. Got to be difficult from the moment the movie began. As the titles were rolling, reddish leaves began tossing around on a green background – leftwards, rightwards. He just didn't feel like watching any of it. A friend on the left let out a wolf-whistle. One other guy chased it. The female friends laughed. The girl on the right laughed too. He didn't even feel like looking up. He would raise his head suddenly, and then immediately let it drop. Huge green fields everywhere, the hero dressed in white shirt and white trousers, the heroine in a white sari, pallu fluttering in the wind. Hero gets hold of edge of pallu and edges closer, closer. It was watchable as far as it went. But when the heroine started racing across all that green dressed in a red sari, that was when he dropped his gaze. Dropped, lifted, dropped, lifted. Movie over. Everybody rose. Knees–arms separated.

Stepping out of the theatre, out now of the gate, it was afternoon. Let's lunch somewhere.

And then at the vada-pao shack nearby, he noticed his Tukaram-quoting friend. Their eyes met. He mumbled something to a girl of the poetry group and crossed over to the shack.

'How about some vada-pao?' said the friend.

'No, not really,'

'Read some Tukaram?' asked the friend with a laugh.

'No, not yet,' he laughed back.

'You're impossible!' said the friend and started off –

By scraping crumbs that others leave
If poet's fame be won
The sinner bideth time in hell
Till turneth moon or sun
Tuka says hold on to God
All else to grief doth run

He laughed. The friend laughed.

'You believe in god?' he asked the friend.

'You believe in alpha beta gamma?' countered the friend.

'Chyaayla, talk straight, can't you? What do you mean alpha beta gamma?' he growled.

'There are those hundred thousand people who swear by this thing called alpha beta gamma, and fifty out of that very crowd come and tell us that there is this thing called alpha beta gamma; so what do you say, you believe?' his friend expounded.

'What d'you mean? What do we have to do with it? I mean, I don't quite understand,' he said, flustered.

'That's exactly it. What do we have to do with it?' the friend said and laughed.

He laughed too.

'You're just a Tukaram guy?' he asked.

Just then, one of his poetry group friends called him.

'I'm a Namdeo guy too,' said the friend.

'Chal, I'll push off. Got to go for lunch. Talk to you later.'

'Yeah, sure. See you.'

He had lunch with the poetry group. By then the movie had drained out of his head.

❖

After his meal that day he felt terribly down. Down to the point that he didn't even want to talk. They were discussing the movie to the high heavens, but he wasn't in it. The girl who had sat to his right in the cinema hall was called Sonal. She was wearing a black shalwaar and a light pink half-sleeved kurta.

Chyaaychi, head is nicely stacked up with girls' clothes, he thought, and squirmed. When he thought of the number of girls whose clothes he knew in such details, he felt further dispirited. So took a plunge and told her, 'You look very pretty today!' She laughed mightily, bosom and all. And she touched him on the hand and said, 'Thank you!'

Sonal visited him in his dreams that night; hair let loose. And he melted below the waist.

Everything was bubbling along. Super. Laughter. Wildness. Swarms of poetry.

There was no difference at all among the three graduation years. Same girls. Same boys. Same bodies. Slightly different but same poems, Slightly different but same clothes. Sonal, however, did give him a grand, excited hug, bosom included, and that stuck in his memory, bosom included. From then on, almost every night it was almost always Sonal who visited his dreams. Whatever clothes Sonali wore, the girl in the dream was always Sonal.

The group went on full-swing with its poetry sessions. They read out to each other. They read out to others. Meanwhile, three pairings happened. Things sailed along with boundless enthusiasm.

❖

Not as enthusiastic as before, but not unenthusiastic either, thirty-year-old he sat in front. I on this side of the table. He on the other side, leaning back in his blue chair. Just a trace of white in his hair. Spectacles. Thin moustache. White shirt, bluish jeans. A hint of a belly. Five feet six inches tall. His gait that of a second rung entrepreneur. The wooden chair in front smooth and beautiful, the polish glistening.

'You know R.D. Karve?' I shot off, quite pointlessly.

He just laughed. I laughed too, mainly at myself.

'Dhondo Keshav Karve was awarded the Bharat Ratna. He worked for women's education and things. His eldest son was Raghunath. He worked on issues related to family planning and sexual freedom. One major stir he created.' Don't know why I brought up just any old subject, so pointlessly.

This is how we generally while away time, talking of irrelevant stuff. Well, then, here I was, coming up with my own pointless stuff.

'When did he live?' he asked.

'Died in 1953.'

Well, if it is only a matter of passing time, one subject is as good as another. I mean, just five minutes earlier, I had read out an sms to him, which went:

There are these two friends.

One tells the other, 'I'm a poet.'

The other, 'I'm deaf.'

Chyaayla, full five minutes we'd laughed over it. And then bang into R.D. Karve.

A post-shower gloom had spread outside the window.

'I've heard the name, yes, don't know anything beyond

that,' he said. With that, he pulled a paan out of a pouch and stuffed it in his mouth. Mouth now tight shut till he got some spittle ready.

I blabbered on.

'Thought maybe you care for subjects like sexual freedom and such stuff, so I brought it up,' I smiled and said.

He and his wife have decided not to have a child. But that really has nothing to do with R.D. Karve. His wife keeps getting fibroids in her ovaries, and he too gets occasional convulsions. So they've decided against having kids.

But we seem to have gone a little too far ahead. This R.D. Karve thing messed things up.

A little little little little back- back- back- backwards.

He is twenty-six. Runs a fabrication business. As he had declared at home and everywhere else, he was getting his Master's degree in Economics. But then, towards the end of the second year, he'd developed a big-time distaste for the entire thing. He had completely run out of interest on the subject. When he went to college, it was only for the poetry and the group. And then he just let it go altogether. Equally suddenly, he teamed up with a friend in his fabrication business. Didn't know head or tail of the stuff, but then he wanted money, and for that he would have to work, like it or not. So he started visiting his fabricator friend, casually like. Soaked up knowledge. Began understanding the finer aspects. Started off on his own. Hired a room for an office in a building. Little by little, work started trickling in. Poetry and the group alongside.

Twenty-three to twenty-six were difficult years. He didn't really register how they went by. There was so much running around that he was hardly conscious of anything else. Hunting out work, meeting builders, bringing in material, organizing the workmen, making trips to sites, getting after people for payments, he got properly trapped. You need money to live, so he really had to focus on work. Poetry and the group happened occasionally.

The work, of course, brought him many benefits. For one, he bought himself a two-wheeler. At age 25, he became the owner of a middle-range bike. The people at home also stopped nagging him. They truly had been nagging him for two years, and that was what had got him working with such frenzy. His father was a proofreader, and his mother was a clerk in the accounts department of a private firm. That's about all there is to say about his people at home.

In spite of being submerged in work, he would now and then find time for poetry and the group. Sonal gave him another enthusiastic hug in one of those meets. The pressure of her breasts pushing through her thick white T-shirt he would remember for the next six months. Their cheeks brushed too, another item worth remembering. It did hurt him, though, however much one might sneak past it, that he could not give as much time to poetry as he could earlier. Three-four of his friends from the group stayed in the college hostel, they had the luxury of being able to stay connected with the world of poetry. He couldn't manage that.

That he could buy himself a two-wheeler brought him another big benefit. He met the person who would in due course become his wife. Her name was Shalmali. She had been in the same class with him at school, but she worked her magic on him in his twenty-sixth year. That was when he had gone to get his bike serviced...

As he stepped out, receipt in hand, after dumping his bike in the garage, he noticed Shalmali walking into the next lane. Bag slung on shoulder. She looked beautiful. He recognized her instantly and called out to her. She looked towards him, a bit bewildered, and broke into a smile.

'Arey, you?' Shalmali said.

'Yup, me.'

'What have you been doing? And how are you? How come here?' Shalmali, wind-blown hair and all.

'How about some tea?' with a small laugh.

A response laugh, and Shalmali said yes. There was a restaurant close by, of course, and they went in. Ordered two cups of special tea.

'Okay, shoot,' he told Shalmali.

Shalmali works at a cooperative bank on the first floor of the building next to where his servicing garage is. She's wearing a yellow kurta and a white shalwaar.

'How different you look!' she laughed and said. Since she laughed all the time, a little less or a little more, no point in repeating this. And because she looked more and more beautiful every time she laughed, no point saying this either. But just for one last time, a half-sleeved kurta, a sparkling white shalwaar, slightly high-heeled sandals, a gold-plated watch on the left wrist, fairish complexion – Shalmali looked bewitching.

He told her about bringing his bike for servicing. About his fabrication work. About his decent earnings. Shalmali listened to it all. He started feeling immense sympathy for her. This was the first time he was feeling thus, without much reason either. Shalmali told him about her circumstances. Nothing seriously out of the ordinary. Middle-class family. Their circumstances rather better than middle-class, really. But the pressure to get married was mounting all the time. People at home were pestering her to pieces. She wasn't laughing when she said this.

Just then the tea arrived, and the subject was dropped.

Shalmali: 'Okay, what more? How are things with you?'

He: 'Oh, getting along, getting along quite well. My work is settling nicely.'

Shalmali: 'Things at school were so different, na?'

They had been together at school ten years ago. Things then and things now were bound to be different!

He laughed.

Shalmali said, 'We never ever talked at school!'

'Well, nobody ever talked at school!'

'You have brother, sisters?'

'No, I'm a single child.'

One full minute sipping the tea.

'How d'you come to office?' he asked.

'By bus.'

Tea over, as they stepped out of the restaurant, Shalmali said, 'I've to get back to office. What time d'you pick up your bike? If you're coming this evening, we could meet. Otherwise tomorrow.'

'That's perfect. What's your mobile number?'

She gave him her mobile number and took his. They walked up to the mouth of the lane. 'Lovely meeting you,' said Shalmali.

He smiled.

'Well, see you, then!' said Shalmali as she turned into the lane. He called out to her. She retraced a few steps. 'You look lovely,' he said. She laughed and said, 'Thanks.'

And then she said, 'These flowers look pretty too, na?'

Oh, shit! Now where the devil are these flowers? He concealed his confusion somehow. Then he noticed a shrub at the mouth of the lane that Shalmali was looking at. He guessed it had to be that, and said, 'Yes, they do.'

'What are these?' he asked

'Kanher,' she said.

And then she left for office. He had to go to a site, so he hopped on to a bus.

In a little while, an sms arrived from Shalmali, 'Loved meeting you. And yes, you looked nice too.'

He sent a reply, 'Hmm. See you this evening.'

From then on, they kept meeting.

They started going for rides. The space between their sittings shrank. The space between their conversations shrank. Their hands began meeting more and more. She told him she loved him. He told her of his confusion between red and green. That stumped her a little bit, and her eyes turned moist. That was the first time she hugged him. She was younger to him by four odd months. She didn't wear glasses. He had begun wearing them recently. They began going for movies every weekend.

During one such movie, out of nowhere, she asked him, 'Do you still remember the wristwatch of the girl at school?

He was stumped. Then he collected himself. Then he remembered. The little finger. He remembered the watch with the brown strap. But how the devil did she know all this?

Shalmali continued, 'You held her little finger, you expressed your admiration for her watch. Well, I was coming down the same stairs then.'

Chyaayla, this was a new spin. Even otherwise, he couldn't get a hang of the movie on the screen. And now this strange little twist. Her face didn't betray a whisper. And bang in the middle of the movie, she had lobbed this one! 'Chhey chhey,' he mumbled, and turned deaf. But then she herself set things straight.

'Oh, just let it go, re, I was just pulling your leg,' she said, and laughed. He remained deaf. She then closed up to him, pecked him on the cheek and moved away. He continued playing deaf.

The lights went on flickering on the screen in front. The colours kept changing. Shalmali sat to his left, and her right hand rested in his left hand.

That very day, right outside the very same cinema hall, he saw his Tukaram friend outside the very same vada-pao stall. Was seeing him after years. But just the same, and right there too. He waved at him, and after a whispered word to Shalmali, crossed over to the stall. The friend laughed, he laughed.

'How's life treating you?' The friend hadn't shaved for some time.

'Good, good. How about you?' he replied.

'Oh, I'm doing okay too. The other day we had left Namdeo hanging.' So saying, the friend started straightaway –

Water bubbles, as you watch,
In the blink of an eye do vanish;

So doth the world as you behold;
It ends with nothing left to hold.
As juggler's tricks thin air become,
So, verily, doth the world.
No good, says Naama, there resides;
Transient are its truths.

He heard the friend out, and then asked him, 'Has any girl ever let you come close to her, a little bit, at least?'

This completely stunned the friend. And then he vanished. Meaning, well and truly disappeared.

He had asked the friend a really simple question, really! And that too in pure fun! But the question caused the friend to disappear altogether! Well, yes, it isn't as if it was altogether such a straight and simple question. He well knew what he possessed and what the friend did not possess, and hence the question.

Finally,

The joys of the bed are gained with the doing;
No telling can ever describe them.
Burn down this word-based knowledge, says Tuka;
The mark of Vithoba the rarest can know.

The friend would certainly know that these lines came from Tukaram. So chances are, the friend would have suddenly been hit by his own ignorance, and so did the vanishing trick. What could he do?

He went back to Shalmali and they set off for lunch.

Two

The light shining on the pen-stand. The yellow light criss-crossing through green and red leaves. The sunshine back into play after the rains. So mild, the sunshine. The street glittered here and there.

The office is his, and he is my friend.

He sat chewing on his paan in front of me.

So pointlessly, again, I said, 'R.D. Karve, however, was a great person.'

He laughed with lips tightly shut.

Then he began playing some kind of a game on his computer. I too just continued sitting there.

The sunshine outside would turn dim occasionally, signalling the drifting in and out of clouds. I started getting bored. The chairs were nice and sturdy. Glistening with polish. Heavy chairs.

The walls of this building too were strong and thick. Grey. His office room was painted off-white. It was a very tiny office. A printer rested in a corner.

Thick dark clouds had again started gathering outside. It would begin raining again, almost certainly.

He felt like just not moving from the chair he was sitting on by the window. Cars coming and going outside. People coming and going.

The window bars were iron, painted grey.

A slow, melancholic precipitation had begun.

He was given a horrible thrashing at a site once. Thrashed to the point of bleeding. This was around the time that he and Shalmali had begun going strong.

It was a Mumbai site. A finance firm. He really hadn't wanted to accept this work, but it had come through an acquaintance, and it was his first big offer. Could well bring in up to five lakhs. Brought in the material. Gathered the labourers. Started the work. Some beams had to be laid at some places. There was some glazing work to do. And some ceiling work too.

Things started off quite well. But when he went there the second time, the manager of the finance firm asked for five thousand rupees. Straight asked. No hiding, no hush hush voice, nothing. Just, 'Pass over five thousand.' This wasn't new to him. He withdrew cash from an ATM and handed it over to the manager.

Once was all right, maybe, but the manager soon made it a bit of a routine. The power would go off, or the water supply would be blocked. Labour complaints started coming in. It was turning messy, although the work went on. The manager once demanded money from the labourers, straight!

He tried lodging a complaint with the manager's superiors,

but that didn't yield any results. And then he told the manager he wouldn't give him any more money. Although he was furious, he didn't say it in so many words. Just told him, 'Can't manage today.' The manager went in, and came out, this time with some four-five others. They all worked with the finance firm.

The manager gave him the first shove. Then the rest began pushing him around and hitting him. On the stomach, on the knees, on the ankles, on the head, a heavy pummelling. The manager's ring also bruised his forehead.

Then they pulled out whatever money he had in his pocket. He was bleeding a little bit at the mouth. His shirt was soiled, a top and a middle button wrenched off. He didn't immediately register the different places that would begin to ache soon. His head was numb. His right hand and right knee were aching. There was blood on his forehead. On his leg too. He was breathing heavily.

Numbly he got up and looked around for some water. The firm's office was located at the end of a narrow lane. He first found his way out of the lane. Next to the chawl on the left was a small tap. He gave his face a splash first. Ran water through his hair. Scrubbed his hands. Removed his shoes and washed his feet. Lifted the trouser legs and washed his knees. He was now regaining his wits. Maadarchod bastards. He straightened his shirt and dusted it. There was this ironing shack alongside. He went and sat there on the iron bench.

The rectangular chawl. Clothes hung out to dry. Saris, shirts, trousers, petticoats, towels. So many colours fluttering in the wind. A kid was riding a bicycle. There was a steady drone of noise. The ironing man asked, 'What happened?'

He told him about the work going on at the finance firm and all, how the manager beat him up and all. The ironing man handed him a bottle of water.

He sat there for five-ten minutes, and started feeling better. He was just very thirsty, otherwise he was fine. He finished the bottle of water, and then started feeling leaky.

Sugam Toilets: By courtesy of the Bruhan Mumbai Municipal Corporation.

He saw the board and went and eased himself there. That's when he regained some sense. The guys had hit him hard. He felt very agitated. And very humiliated.

That day he remembered Jayaraj.

But that requires some travelling back in time.

A little little little little

Back back back back.

He saw Jayaraj driving a six-seater. So Jayaraj was driving a six-seater rickshaw these days! He had just begun getting into his friend's fabrication business. Poetry had reduced due to the pressures of work, but it was going on still. Last he had seen Jayaraj scampering out of college three years ago, and now he met him driving a six-seater. They greeted each other.

Jayaraj has been driving a rickshaw for the past two-three years. He didn't waste his time going to college after the tenth grade. They took each other's mobile numbers. He told Jayaraj about the fabrication work. Jayaraj later also got him a couple of fabrication jobs. He travelled on Jayaraj's rickshaw a number of times; they had tea together too seven-eight times. Not as if they had a lot of conversation, but the bond remained.

Then Jayaraj just disappeared. Some six-seven months later

he read in the papers about his involvement in a murder. He was quite blown away. Within a week of reading this news, he saw Jayaraj. Jayaraj was astride a bike – that was when his own bike was still in the future. They waved at each other.

At first he couldn't fathom, chyaayla, how the devil could he afford to move around so openly? So he went over to where he had halted his bike in front of a paan shop and said, 'Arey, I read the news the other day.'

Jayaraj laughed. Blue jeans, pink full-sleeved shirt, white shoes, bracelet. He, of course, always had a sturdy build. Sat there on a 100 cc Yamaha.

'Aren't you afraid?' he asked.

'What afraid? It's people who fear me.'

That day too they sat and had tea.

They didn't meet often after that. There was little likelihood of such meets anyway.

He remembered Jayaraj the day the finance firm's guys banged him. (Another bit: he even wrote a poem titled 'Macho' on this experience.)

He called up Jayaraj after a couple of days. Told him exactly what happened, and also told him exactly what he wanted him to do.

He just had to do this, and to hell with the consequences. He was absolutely determined that it simply had to be done. He told Jayaraj to come along with him to Mumbai just once. And Jayaraj came too. Just he and Jayaraj. When the finance firm's guys saw Jayaraj, chain round the neck, rings on fingers, they realized just where they stood. Jayaraj also handed the manager a visiting card. There was no need for any explanations. Half an hour, that's it.

From then on, he didn't run into any obstacles at work. The manager didn't return to ask for money. The work got over in a couple of months.

The manager got his revenge though. He was short-changed by about one lakh rupees. But this time he didn't call Jayaraj.

In fact, Jayaraj had told him, 'If you want anybody rubbed out, just say so.' And he had replied, 'If you want anybody rubbed in, just say so.' Later, of course, he found his statement quite corny. But he did put it into verse.

So, he did suffer a loss of a lakh or so rupees, but he saw the job to its end.

This job, however, had made him bleed.

Around this time, he bled another way too. But it took time to register that.

It was during the period that Shalmali had proposed that his piles problem began. Of course, he didn't realize what it was during the early stages. Yes, he would feel the pain while evacuating, but never noticed the blood that went with the stools. Didn't notice the blood, and so didn't understand exactly why all that pain. He thought whatever it was would fix itself. But the pain refused to fix itself; quite the opposite, it went on increasing.

When he finally went to the doctor, the doctor said, 'There are very bad fissures inside.' That was when the piles hassle latched on to him.

He sits, I sit, time really passes easily in this office. Well, really it's time alone that passes the way it does, but yes, we end up feeling good. In fact, even this business of feeling good, actually it doesn't feel at all. And that by itself is good.

It was drizzling a bit again. Occasional vehicles crossing this way and that. Finished the paan in his mouth and asked, 'Call for some tea?'

It was time for tea anyway. Three-thirty. He called up the tea guy. The tea stall is right along the side of the building. They put the compound wall to all kinds of use – for drying clothes, leaning the water pitcher against, lining up the tea glasses on the ledge, hanging bags – they use it quite nicely. The owner of the tea stall is Dhaaya. He ordered tea from Dhaaya over the mobile phone. In five minutes, a kid appeared with a kettle and plastic cups.

Tea in front. Drizzle outside. Pen-stand on the table.

I write about him. He sits in front sipping tea.

Even if he is sometimes confused, he is quite at peace. He had never been so much at peace before. It's only in these last three-four years that this peace had arrived. He would so often be restless earlier.

Shalmali proposed to him, they began moving around together, seeing movies together, meeting for snacks and meals, shopping for clothes.

It was on one such outing for a movie, after the tickets had been bought, that Shalmali suddenly said, 'Let's not go inside.' Straight out of the blue. The tickets had been bought half an hour earlier, and they had gone for some tea; it was while returning, when they were about to enter the gate that she said, 'Let's not go in, please.'

Chyaayla, he felt, what's this new stuff?

'What happened?' he asked.

Shalmali froze. Turned around.

'Hey, but what happened? Not feeling well?' he asked.

'No, you just come along,' she said, and took him to the bike.

They drove a long distance on the bike. They found a place to sit, some stone benches. She calmed down a bit after sitting there for a while.

'What happened?' he asked again.

Shalmali then told him an old story. Not old old really, but from three years ago. She was twenty-four then. That was when a boy had proposed to her. Let's call him 'Hero'. He was good-looking. Worked as an engineer in some firm or the other. He had been together with her in junior college. A slight acquaintanceship had continued. She said she would think over it, meanwhile, they could meet and talk. Hero agreed. She began meeting the boy, chatting with him. Hero told her to wear certain kinds of clothes, and she obliged. Hero told her to sit astride the bike, not with both her legs to one side; she obliged again. Hero told her she looked beautiful, she heard him out and dutifully liked it. Later when they met at a certain place, he asked her to come closer. She dutifully moved into his arms. And that was when she began feeling that she did not like him. Then she cut down her responses to his mobile messages. And then one day she told him, 'I don't think I want to marry you.' Hero got annoyed. She cried. Then Hero cried. After the crying, Hero pulled her close. Now she was dead certain that she didn't like him. They went around for about six-seven months before she brushed him off. Saw five movies during this period. From the very first movie onwards, he held her hand, touched her knee. For some time she liked it very much. But suddenly, one day, she wondered, 'What's going on here?' And then she chucked it all. Hero gave her a piece of his mind. She just went home and cried, and brought it all to a close. She then changed her mobile number.

All this stuff Shalmali narrated to him that day.

What had happened was that on returning to the cinema hall she had spotted Hero, and that had given her a jolt. She had then pulled him away and told him all this.

He was agitated. Hugely agitated. Didn't say anything, but his mind was on fire. Shalmali sensed this. She said, 'Sorry, but it was the first time that somebody had asked me, so...'

'Why didn't you tell me this before?'

'Arey, we've never really talked! And what was there to say?' Shalmali started crying.

'Chyaayla, why do you cry?' he said, got up, went to his bike, started it, and sped away.

And for one full week he and Shalmali didn't meet. She went on sending him messages. 'You are good,' 'You are the one I care for,' 'Sorry!' and so on. He didn't respond to any of them.

Just once he sent her a long message full of questions.

– How many times did you two meet?

– Where all did you meet?

– Where all did he touch you?

– Why do you like me?

And then Shalmali landed straight at his office and just took him in her embrace. He didn't say a word. Don't know exactly what happened to him, but he suddenly started feeling very sorry for her.

'Sorry,' she said again.

'There's a huge difference between you and him, re. It was just that he had asked, and I had to think it over,' Shalmali said.

Again, difficult to say exactly what happened to him, but he started feeling unhappy about himself. He felt he didn't deserve to take this girl in his embrace.

'And I didn't meet him as often as I've met you. I've not let you touch me places, so how, possibly, could I have let him?' Shalmali started crying.

He started feeling bad for both of them now.

Then suddenly he relaxed.

Then suddenly he started feeling free.

His head became light. Didn't feel a thing. Shalmali stayed in his embrace in the office. Hardly an office, that, just a room by the side. There was nobody around. Nevertheless, he pushed the door shut, pulled Shalmali closer to him and pressed his lips upon hers.

She went limp too, and let all her weight fall upon him. He didn't understand what, quite, had happened to her. But she was smiling, ever so softly. And looking straight at him with eyes wide open. He felt bad about himself. But then he thought, well okay, that's it.

She just looked at him steadily.

He then said, 'Okay now, sit here in front.' But Shalmali refused to leave his embrace. Just tilted her head and kept looking at him steadily. Finally, he ran his hand over her back and seated her in the chair in front. She put her head on the table and just drifted into sleep. He pulled out a paan, put it in his mouth, and sat peacefully in the blue chair.

His manner of looking at Shalmali changed entirely from that day on. Don't know whether it was because of his peaceful blue chair, or because he ate paan, or because of his confusion between green and red, but he never ever asked her anything about the episode again.

But on his own, he did think about it. Thought about it at the ground level, and thought about it from Olympian heights. Like, it struck him once, during his college days a girl called Sonal had after all hugged him enthusiastically, twice; and, well, this Hero had embraced Shalmali exactly twice, so accounts squared. Or, like, he had held a girl's little finger in school, where had Shalmali got herself a similar opportunity? In fact, he had not even registered her presence on the staircase! And basically, she actually turned Hero down and actually proposed to him of her own volition, that would mean that she seemed attracted towards him alone, didn't she? But why didn't she tell him earlier? But what bloody difference does it truly make if she didn't?

Then: Sonal didn't really love him, so her embrace of him would be different from Hero's embrace of Shalmali! As a matter of fact, he had embraced only Shalmali in that fashion. And it was because of Hero that they missed the movie. Shalmali did go see movies with Hero, and pulled him out just because she had spotted Hero! And also, what was all that crying about? Chyaayla, could the girl be lying? No, she couldn't be lying. Didn't seem so looking at her eyes. And what would she gain by lying, anyway…?

…It was while these thoughts were swirling in his head that another episode happened.

It happened that he had a friend named Samidha. Senior

to him by three-four years. So she was about thirty. It began as just a casual acquaintanceship, and soon developed into a good friendship. She stayed in the same building in which he lived. And they became good friends. But just friends. After graduating, she was working as a clerk in a firm. She looked nice, but work had brought her into the thirties and she hadn't got married. She was a lone girl at home. But time had just slipped away. It was in this scenario that a man visited her at the firm. Basically, this person had come for some kind of work he had with the firm. That work brought him to her table, and once there, he made deep inroads. Asked for her mobile number. She gave it to him too. That very evening, she received a message from him: 'I want to sleep with you.'

Beat that!

Samidha told him this while they were having tea at a restaurant. The restaurant next to the building they lived in, the very next day after the first message had arrived. He felt like laughing. But Samidha was serious. She next met him after exactly fifteen days. By then she had given herself the pleasure of sleeping with the man. And that too in her own flat. Meaning, in their very own building. And to top it all, she came and told him about it too as they were having tea. The way he got blown off his feet, he never came down as far as this episode was concerned.

The way it unfolded was that on the first day the man sent Samidha that one single message, and came straight to the point. And when he returned to the office for his work on the third day he asked her what she thought about his proposal. She began making inquiries, and learnt that he was a married man. He had a small son too. From the way Samidha talked of him, he was likely to be a good-looking person. She wondered why he had just wanted sex and nothing else. When she asked him, his reply was clear. He just wanted sex, no other involvement of any kind. Any place of her choice would do for him, but he wanted her physically. He would have sent her around a hundred messages putting across his case to her. Her first reply was a straight 'No.' But she then asked him what he thought of her. His response was very clipped, 'I want to sleep with you.' Finally, on the fifteenth day, she indulged herself with that man.

It was quite natural that he would get completely blown off his feet by what Samidha told him. For one, Samidha was a very simple, uncomplicated girl. She still is. Dresses in Punjabi shalwaar-suits or saris. Has never been seen fooling around with anybody. Would have gotten married too. In fact she still may. But she just refuses to subject herself to being 'seen' in the traditional fashion. And as she earns good money, she refuses to back off on many issues. Hence, things haven't moved on for her. This, then, is Samidha. On hearing her out, he was altogether stumped.

To begin with, the first thought that crossed his head was: that bastard's aaichi gaand! And then he was astounded by Samidha. Gosh! She could do this!

Then, along with what a wretched guy that bastard was, he began to think that he himself had had a chance with her and he never knew it! Aayla!

Samidha definitely is pretty. Half an inch or so taller than him. He had known her for so many years, but had never really observed her closely. She was so little a part of his environment that she was not even mentioned in conversations. They knew each other well, yes, and had tea together at the restaurant next to their building. But she had never lingered in his head. Now, after her disclosures, she did begin to linger.

He then began admiring Samidha. Or really, he began feeling bad for her. But then, really, he did really feel great admiration for her. Looked at from her side, she so obviously appeared so totally liberated. He couldn't get a proper handle on the man, though. Look, she just about knew his name, no more. But then he wouldn't carry her over to some odd, unknown place. She asked him to, and he came over to her house. Straight. She didn't even check him out for hidden cameras or stuff like that. He just came in his everyday clothes, that's all. All that she saw was that he was good-looking, or so it appears from her narrative.

It had given him an absolutely novel shock that she could actually have thought along these lines. But a look at her face, and he couldn't understand a thing. He began to feel that the atmosphere had suddenly cleared. Often he wondered whether he too could now tap her. He also wondered whether her relationship with that man was still on. The wretched bastard, and what bloody cheek, he felt. About Samidha, however, he began feeling a great sense of liberation. He took her out to tea whenever they met. But, of course, he did not ever ask her.

(He did write a poem called 'Samidha' on this subject. It went like:
In the teardrops that rested in her eyelids,
Showed the face of sorrow gone melancholic
And so on. But let that be.)

What did emerge from this episode was that Shalmali came out with something from her past. Just around this time, the strange Samidha tangle came to the fore, and he suddenly opened up. He began finding everything clear, tender, unfettered. From that day onwards, his attitude towards Shalmali changed back to being pretty much what it had been earlier. He would occasionally get into a blue funk and suddenly talk bitterly. He would turn suspicious if Shalmali didn't want to visit a certain place. But this too went into a natural decline. It was amazing. Shalmali was amazing.

Three

There's politics in everything.

Somebody has said this, I told him, as we sat in office, and he got a good fix on it.

Paan in mouth. This paan habit, it has become an addiction with him. Habits don't go. Chews at least twenty paans in a day. Must be spending a good three-four thousand a month on it.

The reason I write all this is that I can't see him in pain. He gets convulsions, he can't differentiate between green and red (the traffic signals, however, he has always been able to read, so he's never had any problem since the time he started using a vehicle, which is good). He has piles, his wife has fibroids in the ovaries, so they've decided not to have children. These convulsions are a truly dangerous thing. A guy in his building had one as he was riding a bike. Collapsed on the road, got struck on the head, and went blind. Six months into his marriage, and suddenly struck blind. What could he do?

That's just why, chyaayla, I keep telling him, 'Bhadvya, use a helmet.'

His first epileptic fit hit him when he was twenty-seven. Around the time that he and Shalmali were seeing each other every day. He happened to be at home then. So when his jaw got locked and he turned stiff, the people at home laid him on one side. That was when it was realized that it was epilepsy. He told Shalmali about it the very next day. She felt very sorry for him.

Everything else, however, was moving along. He couldn't properly spot a gulmohar. He didn't even realize the first time round that kanher has flowers. He had to settle for a headache with some Hindi movies. Once, as he held Shalmali's hand, she was wearing two slim bangles, one green and the other red, and of course he hadn't noticed the difference. Noticed when she brought it to his notice. Another time, she wore a green kurta and a red churidaar, his eyes and his head went for a complete toss. Most significantly, he never offered the so-called romantic red rose to Shalmali. It never even occurred to him. The result was that he never had the so-called experiences that so many so-called people had with the so-called world of so-called colours.

Around this time, he got the news of Jayaraj's murder. When he read it in the papers, he went numb for a little while. Jayaraj had been sent across to the other world, 'Macho' tattooed on his biceps and all. The papers carried the detailed news of the murder. Near the temple below the bridge – eight knife stabs and two bullets. Game over. Nothing left to talk about.

He had called up Jayaraj during the finance firm episode.

Then had lost all contact. He had gone into a state where he lost track of so many things. Jayaraj was a worker for a political party. That of course had to happen. But now this, and so quick?

He was his classmate – Jayaraj. Two-three years older to him. The area in which he lived, certain things move along pre-destined lines there. Chyaayla, but Jayaraj dead! Just vanished from the world. He was so numb that he didn't even know how exactly this event had affected him. Jayaraj dead and gone.

And he went and told Shalmali, 'Let's get married.'

His fabrication business was moving along nicely. He'd bought himself a two-room flat in an oldish building half an hour away from his earlier flat. Twenty-seven years of age, he. Got married. Nothing much to say about the wedding ceremony. I wasn't there anyway. He hadn't wanted any big affair either. Called a few persons over and got married. No brassband, no fanfare. To hell with fanfare.

And right after that, within two days, poetry began to seem frivolous.

The first day after the marriage just drifted away, and the next day Shalmali and he surrendered themselves physically to each other with complete, ecstatic abandon. The details, of course, are very private to them. But one thing needs to be recorded. The total absorption that Shalmali brought, he didn't in the same measure. And registered this himself, okay? But that's all right, fine. When they had scaled all those ethereal heights, and lay sated and calm, that was when it struck him that all his time spent on poetry was so much frivolousness. This thought just flashed into his mind and out. Later, they got back to a slow relish of each other's physicalities for a little while. He suddenly started feeling a deep respect for Shalmali. She, on her part, had completely given herself over to him. He found every part of her so bewitchingly beautiful. He was convinced that he had never felt such deep joy and contentment before. Unbounded contentment.

Why did he ever write poetry? Why did he get into recitations at college? Why was there this poetry group? What fundamental purpose did all of it serve? He didn't have to think too much to answer these questions. His resolution the next day: no further poetry. At least as far as he was concerned, from here on, aaicha gho to all poetry.

Shalmali began to lavish all her love upon him. Even more than before. She never spoke crossly with him. Never. Later too the two of them drank deep of the pleasures of each other's bodies. But it was the earlier experience, the first one, that had truly sent poetry packing out of his system.

There were so many things about himself that began surprising him. A number of things had happened without his being consciously aware of them, and now they began appearing increasingly frivolous. Within days of getting a computer and an internet connection in his office, he had created a blog and posted a few poems on it. He had posted a few poems at other places too. He had received responses too: 'Great,' 'Full of feelings,' 'Caught it perfectly in words,' 'Beautiful thoughts,' 'Really deep,' and so on. All of this stuff he began finding boring later, which is to say that as far as he was concerned, they were so much of the same boring stuff. So then one day he just upped and deleted the blog. He would see other blogs, read stuff there, give responses. He did whatever he felt like, and whenever he felt like it. But writing his own poems, it got to be just too boring.

It was as if he enjoyed doing all this. He felt as if a huge burden had been shaken away.

Looked at another way, he is under more stress than before. They decided not to have children, the family didn't like that at all. All those neighbours, acquaintances, and relatives and all their intrusive queries! Besides, he gets those fits. And Shalmali has fibroids in her ovaries. He has his piles problem too. Shalmali occasionally has problems during her menstrual periods too. All this has been going on for the past three years. No change at all. Their hassles haven't increased; they haven't decreased either.

We've known each other for three years now and sit in his office killing time. It's during this time-killing that I've written this. There's no count of the number of paans he has chewed during this period. But then, he has never been able to keep such counts. He doesn't take very big fabrication contracts either. Once, earlier, he had taken a contract for a toll booth. But now he just doesn't take on that size of work. He prefers smaller work. The money is good. Shalmali has her job too. What he now most wants is time for himself.

He and Shalmali have never appeared to be unhappy at all. On the contrary, the verdict refuses to arrive on whether one should feel happy or worried about the two of them. He feels good about having given up poetry. But the question now is what he should do with so much of the time that lies unutilized. Then again, for two-three months at a stretch sometimes, he does not take on any real work. Just comes to office and sits. Browses the internet and sits. Eats paan, drinks tea, has his food. Shalmali and he go for jaunts. They have now got into the habit of imbibing rum. They sit and down two-three pegs once in a while. The habit first began with him. Shalmali got in to wean him out of the habit, and herself got stuck. Both of them feel nice and light after a drink. They have stayed away from whisky and beer. They gave those two drinks a shot too. But whisky made them feel down in the dumps, and beer made them feel a little too excited. They didn't want either of the two states and so settled on rum. Whenever they are in the mood for it, he carries the stuff home and they sit and drink.

Quite a similar thing happened with paan. Instead of becoming a bugbear for her, the paan habit sucked her in too.

It's just a two-person household – Shalmali and he. Their building is outside the city; that is to say, the city hasn't reached there yet. So, in effect, they are a good long distance away. Takes them three-quarters of an hour minimum to commute. So he travels across those three-quarters of an hour to come and sit in the office. Takes a detour if he has some site to visit. So this is how life is moving along for him. But what I am afraid of is: what if within these forty-five minutes he has a fit while on the bike? It's going to be bloody difficult! Remember the guy in his building who took a knock while on the bike and got blown away? Went blind, the poor bastard. So then, yes, any stupid thing can happen. And that's exactly why I keep nagging him to start using a helmet. What more can I do beyond nagging, anyway? (One of the questions that bugs me is: have I got into writing all this because I can do nothing else?)

His giving up on writing poetry was a really nice thing to

have happened. One fever less to rack his head; one fever less for Shalmali's head too, very likely.

There are plenty of other nice things too that have happened. He and Shalmali enjoy each other physically to their heart's content. And knowing that they are not looking for any outcome from their physical indulgences helps them enjoy each other without the burden of public expectations. As a result, there are a number of things, in fact, that he enjoys without carrying the load of ridiculous expectations. Like, for instance, he has given himself the joy of buying a heavier vehicle, heavier in weight and heavier in cost, no expectations attached. He gives better salaries to his workmen without worrying about expectations. The fibroids that keep forming in Shalmali's ovaries, he doesn't sit praying that they do not turn out malignant; he doesn't sit thinking about them at all. And it's not as if he has arrived at this behaviour pattern after lots of deliberation. It has happened unconsciously, slowly, over the past three years. Impossible to ferret out why it happened. What's it expected to lead to, anyway, all this ferreting?

But this is amusing. The manner in which he has slowly acquired liberation from so many things is truly amazing. He is still stuck with his paan habit, undoubtedly, and he does want to kick it. In fact, he wants to kick his fancy for rum too.

He sometimes feels that he has lived enough and more. And then he gets confused with this thought. At the age of thirty, how the hell can one ever say that one has had enough of living? In fact, whatever the age be, how, basically, can anyone ever say that it's been enough of living? So, therefore, what he should give up and what he should not is really for him to answer. But helmet he should wear. And I strongly believe that he should understand that confusion is at the root of all being. I realize, of course, that this is getting to be heavier and heavier philosophy. So I'd better stop.

But merely saying that I'd better stop doesn't mean that it's all stopped. Here's his office. The pen-stand with its green and red leaves is right there in front. Out there it is dark. The wind keeps breezing in and out. And he sits there in front, stretched out in his deep blue chair. Sitting there peacefully. What else does one want?

Second Context

One

Her name is Saavali. The name Saavali is not common among Marathi people. But her father was a fan of somebody or the other in the Bengali theatre, and that theatre person had a daughter named Saavali or something, so he named his own daughter Saavali too. And she is dusky by complexion too, saavali. Dusky Dusky – Saavali.

Twenty-eight-year-old Saavali lives alone. Matter of fact, one may say that she lives alone in the town. But of course, it is a rather meaningless statement, because there are people in the town, and, well, there are things in the house too.

It's now been seven months since she came to this town as a lecturer. There's a university here. It's about half an hour away from where she stays. In the early days, she had checked out the possibility of living closer, but as time went by, she found herself liking the house. Got used to it. She's got used to living alone too.

She has an elder brother. He's married and all that, and her parents live with him. So she has just these close people, but it's not as if they hover over her all the time. They did before. They worried about her till she was twenty-six/twenty-seven. They wanted her to get married. But it just went on getting delayed, and then she suddenly cleared the qualifying examination for becoming a lecturer, and there was a vacancy in the university, and she jumped at this opportunity to get away. Felt freed. It wasn't something that the people at home were going to like, but she just moved out anyway. And then they stopped worrying about her, because they don't phone her all that often now. In the four months that she was here, she had received one call, when she was informed of a son born to her brother. She felt very happy. The people at home, of course, were very happy. Later, she had made a trip to Mumbai. She doesn't receive very many calls now. Once in fifteen-twenty days, maybe, and that frequency has been steadily falling. And she's nicely come to terms with it. She would have been furious earlier, but that's not how she feels now.

She has settled down nicely in this house. The first semester at the university got over and she skipped going home saying she had papers to evaluate.

This is the house she loves now. Got it on rent. She had a friend in the town; she got this house through his connection. The owners had left for some foreign land or the other, and the house had been lying vacant, and that was how she had landed it. The friend has left town too, but he did fix this house for Saavali to live in. She very keenly wants to own a house of her own. That time will come whenever it does; meanwhile, she has taken to this house as her own, and the house has returned her affection in equal measure.

It's an old, run-down house. Just three rooms, but big ones. A square hall as one enters, a door across it at the left corner. Immediately beyond the door is a kitchen on the left and bedroom on the right. Toilet and bathroom in the same corner. The bedroom lies unused. She doesn't use it at all. There's no furniture inside it either, except for an old cot. There's a fan and a bulb inside. Her movement is predominantly restricted to the hall and the kitchen.

The dearest place for her in this house is the grill door. The kitchen is to the left as you pass the hall. But there's a step straight ahead, down there, there's a step, and you get to the grill door. This door is permanently closed. Why call it a door? It's a gate, really, but she prefers to call it a door, and that's what she does. It's all open, open for good. There's a lock on one side of it, so yes, that way it is closed. But the grill is so open, its bars are so far apart, that in effect, it's really open. It lets the wind in, it lets the sun in, it lets the air in. She's of course afraid that it would let in a snake or something too, but that hasn't happened yet.

Saavali stands at the door to brush her teeth every morning. There's bare land in front. No house on either side. A patch of green, and trees beyond that. A few feet to the left is a road (the one that goes past her house can be seen here, a little to the left.) Standing there and brushing her teeth makes Saavali get a feel of the morning. If she rises a little too early, she gets there when the very early morning sun reaches there, and stands at the door. Saavali – shadow. She loves watching her own shadow, shadow's shadow. Locks her hands behind and stands, Saavali, or with just one hand behind, when she is brushing her teeth.

Saavali lives in this rented house, but she really loves this house now. Her days have fallen into a routine. Leaves home around ten, walks up to the main road, catches a bus or a six-seater to the university, stays there till about five or six, and back home. This is the burden of her work.

In the early days she was keen on buying a TV. But later she thought a laptop would be a better buy. A laptop would be useful for many more things. She had a fancy for TV from very early childhood. As a kid she was always locked to the TV. It wasn't like she knew what she would be watching there. That is to say, it wasn't as if there was a specific serial or some such thing that she necessarily had to see every day. Saw lots of movies. All kinds of movies and songs. But once she went to college, this reduced.

Why she had been obsessed with TV, Saavali can't quite remember now. It could be because the place where they stayed didn't have enough people her age. Or it could be some other reason. But if one were to say that she was a TV addict, one wouldn't be wrong. The cable arrived when she was in the fifth grade, and then it began raining channels. Oh, the number of channels that kept coming! 24 hours of movies and songs and stuff, on and on. There were just two channels to begin with – Doordarshan and DD Metro. She didn't even know that they got DD Metro only because they lived in Mumbai, and at other places it was just Doordarshan. She was amazed when she first got to know of it. She recalled her amazement when she arrived in this town and found that she could see all the channels here. How different things were around fifteen years ago, she thought, and how things have changed now! Well, she had been susceptible to surprise then over trivial things; she is not so susceptible now. So, anyway, she decided on a laptop. Combine that with the internet, and there you are! The TV would just walk into it, pictures, songs and all. Just two months into her job, then, and she bought herself a laptop. It was great that she was earning so much that in two months she could put together thirty thousand for it.

Compared to where other people of Saavali's acquaintance were, she was getting along quite nicely. A lecturer at the university means good money and no tension. Her subject was Political Science, but she had no illusions about herself. True, she was very good in studies. In spite of all the TV she watched from school days onwards, she always managed good marks. She knew exactly how to take care of her studies. While in the eighth grade, she had worked out that all these studies, these examinations, the examination questions, they were the things for her; that was the road along which she would travel. So she focused on learning what books had to offer, and always got good marks. This she continued to do right till she got herself a Master's degree. Her strategy was validated when she got past the qualifying examination for lecturers too. But one thing she knew for certain: her kind of studies was not the real thing. This of course didn't occur to her while she was in school, but it did, bit by bit, while she was in her Master's programme. She wasn't in Mumbai for her MA; she was in Pune. Two years.

Despite all her studies, she could not have written ten sentences on Ram Manohar Lohia. And when a smart-looking boy had asked her this very question, she had felt embarrassed. And, quite pointlessly, he had rattled out ten things about Lohia for her. He had then sat haranguing her, not just about Lohia, but about the rottenness of the entire university education system. What exactly had got into him she could not fathom.

Saavali wondered why the boy was so hung up on Ram Manohar Lohia. But he looked nice, that boy. He came from some god-knows-where place. She liked him, but she was rather diffident about getting into direct conversations with him. It wasn't as if he had said anything intended to insult her; but right through the two years of the course, she could never work out how she should initiate a conversation with him. She sometimes felt that she would disturb him by talking, and so she held back. Once, when he told her, 'You have a lovely name, Saavali,' she came very close to putting her arms round his neck. But, of course, she didn't do any such thing. She just didn't know how he would have taken it. What could he be thinking about all the time?

She got herself a laptop and her evenings were nicely sorted. It had been a big problem: what to do after returning home from the university. Well, that was quite nicely resolved. The tiffin arrives around nine. Till 9 o'clock, then, and post dinner till she went to sleep, she now had a handy pastime. She remembered this word: 'pastime'. The boy who had talked to her about Lohia had given her this word, and she remembered it after buying the laptop. So she named her laptop 'Pastime'. This was an old habit of hers, giving names to things. And she always wanted these names to be exclusive.

She's gone and given a name to this house too: 'Darkness'. The darkness is only in the inner rooms, but it seems to so suggest its presence all over the house that she thought it would be an appropriate name for the entire house. Initially, she thought the name was a little too pessimistic, perhaps, but by and by it occurred to her that there was nothing pessimistic about it. Even otherwise, when she stands in the morning at the grill brushing her teeth, the golden light does spread inside, and that's undeniable. So there should be no problem with the name. She went ahead, then, with naming the house 'Darkness'.

The laptop made passing time very easy. The first thing she did was to begin using the internet extensively. Started browsing Facebook. And time passed well. Otherwise, passing time in this town would have been difficult.

There's lots of dust here, and moong-bhajias and sev-curry. The dust doesn't bother Saavali, and the moong-bhajias she's begun to love. She hadn't known of the existence of this snack; she first got to eat it after arriving here. As for sev-curry, wow! She loved these two things of the town. There were other such things too.

Saavali loved the university campus too. Besides, she's begun to like a lecturer from the English Department of the university too. But this liking she wants to confine to observing from a distance. His name is Saumya. What kind of a name is that? But then she got to know that his family is originally from Bengal, which came over here long ago and settled somewhere. Looks very young. What would his age be? He's taller than her, and slightly fairer. Tucks his shirt in. His cheeks look smooth. She likes looking at him, but she just doesn't know what she would say if she ever met him. The English department is quite close to hers, so she sees Saumya quite often.

Saavali sometimes feels very lonely. Then she pulls out her laptop and sits watching other people's profiles. Some of her married friends have posted photographs with their husbands; she sits watching them. She enjoys this. But she has never felt like posting even a simple photograph of hers. She is not at all bad looking. She stood before a mirror once to check herself out. Quite presentable, yes. Five feet two inches. Colour dusky. Not too thin, not overweight either. Good hair. A touch of brown there. With a spot of kaajal her eyes look beautiful, is what she thinks. Although she found herself beautiful in the mirror, she didn't feel like posting her picture on Facebook, not then, anyway.

Once, however, one of her college friends had posted an old group photograph of seven, Saavali being one of the group. One of them had commented, 'Hey, Saavali looks so beautiful! Where's she these days?' She loved reading that, hit 'Like', and told them about her job at the university. Those who hadn't known about her move congratulated her. She has lost contact with a large number of them. So many of her friends had gotten married, and then their calls and messages had gradually ceased. Now, with this Facebook, she's managed to resume contact with a few of them.

Saavali has had a rather wide variety of friends, really. So many of her Pune friends would express surprise at the simplicity of her lifestyle, despite her being a Mumbai girl. But then, a large number of her Mumbai group were quite like her. She didn't know now where they all had drifted. A rare one among them would give her a rare call till about two-three years ago. Now, of course, almost nobody calls. There's this friend of hers from Pune. She does send her messages.

Makes Saavali feel nice. She's bought herself a good mobile too. The earlier one was very basic.

A Mumbai girl, so how come so simple? A good many of those that posed this question had this long-distance notion of Mumbai. She didn't know how exactly to describe things to them. She would make the effort, however, and tell them that she lived in a chawl, a two-storeyed chawl; theirs is a house with two small rooms and she told them that so many people who lived there in similar tiny accommodations were quite like her. That, of course, did not mean that every single one of her friends from there was as simple as she was. But there certainly were some, some simple girls like her, she would tell her Pune friends.

And oh yes, she still gets messages from some of the very few male friends she had. One of them upset her so much once that she stopped talking to him. When this boy's marriage was due to happen, he began calling her and asking, 'Should I search out a person for you? Should I talk to your people at home? There's a guy I know,' and things like that. She just couldn't fathom why this fellow should suddenly show so much concern for her. Initially, she would just laugh it off and change the subject. But when he persisted, repeating the same stuff over and over again, she just cut the line one day and never answered his calls again. He then sent her an apology message. But her anger did not subside.

There had been a similar episode with one of her female friends too. She too would pester Saavali about getting married. Earlier, the girl would talk about her own hopes and desires, about the kind of husband she wanted. She would cry, she would bubble with excitement. At first, Saavali made efforts to show understanding, but by and by boredom set in. She continued, however, to hear her out. And then, suddenly, the girl found somebody and then immediately started selling to Saavali the vital importance of marriage and so on. Saavali stopped taking her calls too. She received a message from this friend once but ducked with a 'loaded with work' response. How do people change so much?

When Saavali started feeling lonesome, she remembered her classmate, the boy who had talked to her about Lohia. The word 'lonesome' too she had got to know about from him. Once, during her MA programme, she had to name a purse she had just bought. For no reason whatsoever, she asked him to suggest one, and he came up with 'Lonesome', don't quite know why. She'd felt a little sad on hearing the name. She didn't say anything to him, though. Even otherwise, she didn't talk much with him. But now, in this town, as she sat feeling lonesome, she suddenly remembered him, that's all.

This memory neither thrilled nor saddened her. She just felt a tiny bit melancholic, and that too for a moment. But there are some memories that cause her deep anguish even now.

This was when she was a kid. Saavali came back home early from school. She was very likely in the sixth grade. She could return home alone. The school was very close by. Her school got over early on Saturdays then. So she got back home and was preparing for her afternoon nap. Her routine when she returned early was quite fixed. She would go collect the house keys from the neighbouring room, unlock the door, shake out some chiwda or something from the can onto a largish plate, and sit munching. After tucking in, she would drink a lot of water and go to sleep. That day, however, she came back with an upset tummy, and so she ran towards the toilet. As one comes out of the house, there are three rooms to the left beyond which is a small passage linking the next block. Cross this passage and turn left, and there are the three toilets assigned to her floor in the chawl.

Saavali dumped her satchel at home, latched her house from the outside, and set off towards the common toilets with a bucket. Afternoons are usually quiet times in the chawl. Saavali crossed the passage and turned left. And there she saw a man from a lower floor standing in front of her, dressed in a loose pajama and a white vest. As Saavali proceeded, the man stretched his arms across, as if to block her passage. She first thought that he was joking or something, but then he pushed her violently towards the corner. Saavali lost her balance and toppled against a bucket. She was completely stunned. The man had let his pajamas slip down to his ankles. She saw him naked from waist down with his organ dangling. Her head began to swim. She was scared out of her wits. Just couldn't think of what to do.

Then she started sidling towards the passage ever so cautiously. She could see the man standing with his pajamas down and a smile playing on his face. Baap re! The man did not move forward, just stayed in his corner with his pajamas down. As she slowly inched towards the passage she turned round and her eyes started streaming heavily. Saavali quickly scampered across the passage and raced into her house. Undid the latch, got in, banged the door shut, sat down leaning against the couch and cried and cried and cried. Cried loud and cried deep. Exhausted, she drifted into sleep.

It was horrible.

Why that man would have behaved thus Saavali does not know. Afterwards, whenever she spotted him, she would run and hide. He had a wife and two grown-up sons. She avoided even having to cross his rooms.

As she grew older, the horror receded. But whenever it came to mind, she shuddered. She often wondered if her fear would have disappeared if she had told someone about it during childhood. But who could she have spoken to? There are certain things whose import one gets only when one is older. When she began menstruating, it did not even occur to her mother to explain these things to her in a cool manner. She subdued her anxieties little by little and learnt this fact of life on her own. When it first began, her mother just handed her some rags; later, Saavali began buying sanitary napkins on her own. Such being the state of affairs, who could she have talked to about what happened in the corner of the other side of the passage? Besides, she would be so overcome by shudders whenever it came back to her that talking about it would have been impossible anyway.

Later, when a friend of hers took her hand in his, she thought of that episode and began crying so hard that the boy got scared. Saavali, however, never talked about that incident.

There were many such experiences later. When she grew older she started keeping a pin in her purse for delivering a prick if ever she felt that somebody was trying to probe her. It became a habit with her, and Saavali eventually stopped thinking about it.

She began thinking about it again because of this boy she had encountered during her MA days. Once she felt that he was eyeing her as she sat having tea. She looked back at him and didn't find anything abnormal there. But just for the fun of it, she asked, 'What are you looking at?' And he answered, 'At your throat.' But his glance was so soft that Saavali actually liked it. Since then she has slowly started entertaining thoughts in these areas. But then she would get thoroughly confused and start crying.

Saavali is now quite engrossed in the curriculum. There are barely twenty students or so. It's wonderful that she has become a lecturer. She gets along very well with the students too. During these seven odd months she has been to movies with them four times. There are twelve girls and eight boys, or some such figure. It's probably because of her age, but the students are quite relaxed with her. While teaching too she keeps strictly to the book, so she won't stumble. She is sharply aware that she hasn't done any serious studies on her subject beyond her course books. Now that she has a laptop, she goes online, locates some good articles in sundry journals and magazines, and keeps adding to her understanding of her subject. Saavali felt that she should also raise queries with the boy who had talked to her about Lohia, but she didn't have his number. Searched for him on Facebook, but no luck there either.

Saumya, however, was on Facebook. He sent her a friendship request and she accepted, naturally. But she just couldn't communicate much through Facebook and other such channels. However, she did hit 'Like' on two or three newspaper articles he had shared.

Saavali loved the organized manner in which Saumya lived. She herself was an organized person, but she felt, on almost a daily basis, that she was not as well organized as he was. And the name Saumya, oh, she loved it like nothing else!

When she menstruates, she develops an aversion to everything. Just doesn't want anything at all. She's had this problem since the time she first began menstruating. She visited a doctor once when she was in school, and he suggested that the problem would go away with marriage.

It's not as if everyone goes through the same kind of pain, but with Saavali it's really bad. For three days she wants to cut herself off from everything else. Curses herself for being born a girl. Feels as if someone is pummelling her stomach. On the first day the pain is severe: stomach, waist, back. On the second day it subsides a little bit, and on the third day it is the least, but she knows no ease for three days. She goes to the department, laughs, teaches, but she so wants to get away from it all. By now, however, she's got so used to it that she hardly has anything new to say about it. The pain is there, so it's there, so lump it for three days!

But now, more than ever, she wants to be rid of it. Reason? The other day, on her very first day of menses, she got the opportunity to have a meal together with Saumya. Without any occasion at all, they ate together. Saavali goes to the canteen every day and takes a rice plate. That day, around 2 o'clock, she was having her meal, and suddenly he materialized in front of her, plate in hand. He then asked, 'Can I sit here?' And they ate together.

Saumya got her to introduce herself, introduced himself, and they chatted away through the meal.

She was quite thrilled to hear him speak Marathi. With the name he had, she hadn't thought he could speak the language so well. But when she heard him speak so fluently she loved it, and she smiled. 'You have a lovely smile,' he said. That was when Saavali got into the habit of looking at the mirror every day.

She remembered an episode from long ago. This was around the time she was graduating. She was riding pillion on her friend's bike. That was when the friend said, 'Why don't you use some cream for your complexion?' That's to say, the friend was asking why she didn't use some cream to become fairer. He was a close friend. Close enough for their other friends to tease them about each other. But how could he say such a thing? And Saavali didn't say a thing. It was now that she suddenly remembered the episode. It was so stupid, what the friend had said. How could she ever have listened to it all? The guy had said a few other things too. Had asked why she didn't go to a gym to improve her figure! When she remembered all this, she was livid. But where was the point in turning livid now? When he once cribbed about the mounting petrol expenses for his bike was when she stopped going out with him. But the seriousness of all that the guy had said occurred to her when Saumya complimented her for her 'lovely smile'. But again, what's the point of it all occurring to her now? And no point in feeling bad about not having felt bad then either. And then she forgot it all. She did feel, however, that the guy should not have taken her hand in his. No point feeling that either. She would, however, sit with complete decency on the bike, she remembers; nothing objectionable there, feels Saavali. Well, let her.

Since that day, Saumya started smiling at Saavali. Took her number, and now sends her messages. They chat on

Facebook too.

Saumya has nobody in this town. His house is in Pune. He's taken a flat on rent. Came to the English department two years ago. He loves watching Hindi movies, and goes for a new one every Friday. Doesn't get along with the people at home, and so has found this distant town. It's a small town, but it's nice and quiet. For the rest, it's a railway junction, and that's nice too. He loves to travel. He's been around many places in the country. He speaks English, Bangla, Marathi and Hindi well. Can understand Odiya too. He is twenty-nine years old.

'Didn't fall for a single girl in so many years?' Saavali asked him once as they sat having their lunch.

Saumya laughed and said, 'Oh I did, I did. Fell for two, at least.'

'So?'

'So nothing. One turned down my proposal, and the other did accept, but it fizzled out.'

'Fizzled out?'

'Yeah, I mean, after six months or so she just stopped communicating.'

Saavali went on eating.

'And oh yes, I now have a third one,' said Saumya.

'Who?'

'You.'

This happened just yesterday, and Saavali just didn't know what to say. Saumya smiled. Lunch got over. Day got over, and today has dawned. Saavali still doesn't know what to tell him. He hasn't come up with any further statement. Just that he likes her. But Saavali spent a little more time in front of the mirror. She has put on a light pink kurta and a white shalwaar, her favourite outfit.

Saavali feels very run-down today. Saumya said so much yesterday and today he was nowhere to be seen. She sat in a six-seater and travelled home through the dust. She had bought herself some moong-bhajias from a push-cart. She could have stood by the bhajia-seller and eaten them right there, but that's okay only when there's company. She would have invited stares if she had done it alone, and that she didn't want. So she got them packed. It's after a long time that she is eating moong-bhajias.

Saavali put on songs on her laptop, chucked her dupatta to one side and sat munching on the moong-bhajias. Terrific stuff, this. Tiny little bhajias, crisp. Saavali carefully put on songs that she loves. *Jiyaa laage naa; tere bina mera kaheen jiyaa laage naa'* (Nothing holds any charm when you're not there). She's created a folder of such songs. Romantic ones. She put on those ones. Switched on the ceiling fan. Picked the bhajias one by one and popped them in her mouth. Loving it. She's rolled up her hair and clipped it on top to keep strands from blowing into her face.

She can't get Saumya out of her mind. Nice boy, Saumya. Should I call him over for some moong-bhajias? Will he come?

She's decided to have a bath. She used to come home and take a bath every evening, but it had stopped for the past few months. Today again she felt like her evening bath. To have the songs reach her in the bathroom, she brought a table over to the door inside and placed the laptop on it. There were some Marathi songs in the folder too: *'Tu evhaa tashi, tu tevhaa ashee; tu baharaanchya baahoonchi; Tu tevha tashi'*. (You're sometimes this, and sometimes that; you of the spring, you of the lovely arms! You sometimes this.)

Saavali suddenly begins feeling cold. During her bath too she thought of Saumya. She put on a light dress and came over to stand at the door. Loose white kurta and loose black shalwaar. Light as a feather Saavali standing at the grill door. The evening sun. The evening light does not fall on the grill as the morning one does. The sunlight could be seen dying on the patch of grass. Saavali stood there listening to the songs, and the sunlight slowly disappeared. Went over to the kitchen and set the milk for heating for a cup of coffee. Shifted the laptop to the bed and sent Saumya a message: 'I like a boy too.' And there, in five minutes, was his reply: 'Not really! Who?' Saavali replied: 'You.' Prompt came the reply: 'Great!'

From that day on, Saavali and Saumya began coming closer to each other.

Two

Saumya is coming today, and Saavali is trying to clean up the inner bedroom too. Tomorrow is Sunday. Most of the house has already been set right. The hall has been set right. The kitchen is quite decently fixed anyway. Saavali got into the bedroom. Switched on a bulb there after a very long time. She's begun by sweeping all the muck out. There's a small trunk too under the cot. Had never noticed it before. It was quite light. She just pushed it aside and cleaned out the mess from under the bed and the rest of the empty room. Then she took a wet rag and gave the room a preliminary mop. Mopped up the trunk-top too. Then she sprinkled water on the floor and gave the room another mop. Then she switched the fan on full speed, pulled out the trunk, and opened it.

There are papers inside, tattered, old, yellowed. She rummaged through it. The papers were more or less the same size, very loosely held together. She brought the papers out and tried to arrange them in a stack. There were two books, also old, bound in hard covers. She kept the two aside. There was another book with a red cover. *Lalit Leni: Ram Manohar Lohia* – a Marathi translation of his articles and speeches.

She instantly thought of her MA classmate. Never got to know where he had drifted off to.

There was something scribbled on the paper, but it wasn't easy to decipher. There was some turmeric wrapped up in another piece of paper. The turmeric got Saavali thinking of her grandmother. Granny passed away some seven-eight years ago. Granny didn't have as much as a pair of slippers of her own. And there was a big white patch right in the middle of her forehead, the result of years of kunku applied there. The patch wouldn't be visible earlier, but once grandfather passed away, that is four-five years before granny died, she had stopped applying kunku, and the patch became visible. The kunku must have covered it up earlier. She would feel very strange looking at granny. When she was very young, Saavali would chatter away with granny. But as she aged, granny began turning silent, and the silence stretched on and on. She remembered her granny-without-her-own-slippers when she saw the turmeric. Saavali remembered seeing once, when she was a child, granny take turmeric roots and grind them to powder. There was something tattooed on granny's forearm, something that Saavali could never decipher. But towards the end of her days granny would spit on the tattoo and keep trying to rub it off. She could have been doing this scrubbing from much earlier, which could be why the tattoo was never clearly decipherable. Towards the very end, granny would constantly try to peel off the wrinkled skin carrying the tattoo mark. Later, she started turning dopey. Dopier and dopier till she just faded out. Nobody had any inkling. It was when she didn't get out of her foetal posture to get out of bed one day, when the sun had been up for a while, that people got to know.

Saavali was quite small when granny last spoke. She kept growing as granny kept turning speechless. That's why Saavali has little memory of granny talking. Or was it that granny never spoke? And she didn't have her own slippers either.

What was scribbled on the pages? A number of pages carried the names of various plants, and stories associated with them, or so it seemed. Saavali was not interested in them, so she kept them aside. And there were poems on three of the pages. They went thus:

First poem:

Why has this sunshine
Seeped into my head?
The tagar tree outside blooms in my brain

It's this dust I want
The dust that coats me all over
I myself am dust

In dust will spread roots
And then will proliferate
Sun trees

The sun trees will burst into blossoms again
As the tagar outside
Or the tagar in my brain
Green leaves white blossoms and ashen dust
Will sway with the wind

Solitary but happy
Will sway with the wind
The tagar flowers in my head

Second poem:

All all alone and lonesome
In all the world the lonesomest house and I alone
Alone I in the lonesomest house in all the world

The sun: lonely or lonesome or all of it?
The mere being of the sun
Not lonely not lonesome not all in all
Just being

The sun percolating in the lonesomeness inside
And then my joining with the sun

The yellowish sun coming in as company
Pulling me close
And
Then sun and I becoming one
And yet again the romping with the sun
The tumult in the darkness of the lovely sun
Deep inside me deep inside

Third poem:

The world disdaining
All hot and straining
I dug a pit
Nor cared a bit for loss
And deep inside the pit
Abide the roots

They sprout
And up and out
Then shoots
And leaves
And soon a train of flowers
Travel back to world

The world then plucks
And ravishes
The flowers stems and leaves and all
Screams and curses stream

But I untamed
Back in the pit

Saavali read the poems and got a trifle bored. A lot of it she didn't understand. Then she felt a little afraid too. She also felt that the name 'Darkness' wasn't a good name for the house, after all. It was just a small joke. But no, the house shouldn't have that kind of a name. Cancelled. She renamed it 'Sunshine'. The morning sunshine does get in through the grill, so the name fits, she thought. But what was wrong with the name 'Darkness' anyway? But then, no, not that name. Not this evening, at least.

Who could have written those poems? The person who owned this house? Somebody related to him? To hell with it, why should it matter to her? But the person who owns this house has almost never lived here. The person in whose bank account she deposits the rent lives outside the country. He has never lived in this house. One of the close relatives lived here; could the person have been living alone? Could this person have done all the dealings on behalf of the owner? Two years before she took over, there had been tenants here; could one of them have been a loner here, poor soul?

Saavali now felt like she was going to cry.

She came and sat in the hall. Thought of opening the laptop, but didn't. She just sat and cried herself out. Getting to be nightfall now, why did she have to read all that depressing stuff? But then she tried to think it out a little calmly. Why the crying? What is causing the fear? Good to jot down the issues. As she got up to fetch a pen and paper, her dinner arrived. It comes around eight-thirty in the evening. The caterer woman's boy came and delivered the meal.

Saavali deposited the box in the kitchen and returned to the hall. She didn't feel like crying now, but tense she continued to be. She quickly finished her dinner and got ready to retire.

Three

Saumya will be coming today. Saavali is happy. He's due to arrive at ten. She's finished her bath. The shampoo smells lovely.

She got to know of his arrival by the sound of his bike. He owns a big Enfield. Saavali peeped out of the window as he was removing his sunglasses. He was in blue jeans and a reddish T-shirt. The sturdiness of his body had not been evident in shirt and trousers. She opened the door before he could ring the bell. Saumya smiled and walked in.

This meet finished off with just moong-bhajias and coffee.

They had a number of such meets and grew closer and closer to each other. Saavali began riding pillion with him on the Enfield. What noise this vehicle makes, dub dub dub dub! The smoke behind would be kicking up a lot of dust too! Saavali went on to tell him to buy a new bike too! And Saumya will buy one too! Later some time.

Saavali and Saumya have been steadily growing closer. He

often drops her home on the motorbike.

Saavali's house is a nice meeting place for them. It's a rented house. Can it be bought? Well, inquiries can be made, it's there in Saavali's head. It might be difficult, though. We'll see. What happens will happen. For now, at least, Saavali can call Saumya over, and they can chat and have coffee in peace.

She doesn't feel the same fear that she had felt when Saumya had come home for the first time. In fact, she's got used to having Saumya close by. After having declared their liking for each other, neither has returned to the subject again. They go around together, and that's statement enough. Neither of them felt like having to put anything in words.

And later, after a Sunday morning, the process of forgetting the horrible childhood episode in the passage began for Saavali. In fact, the process of forgetting a lot of unpleasant episodes began from that experience.

First of all, if one wants to get to the finer details of when Saavali started getting closer to Saumya, one would need to examine the first time she sat on his bike. Because that was when she placed her hand on his shoulder, and she was impressed. Good broad shoulders. It was on the bike again that he had to apply the brakes rather suddenly, and her face touched his nape. Then too she felt like getting real close to him. But the process of forgetting the childhood episode in the passage began with the experience that follows –

'Don't go,' she told Saumya one Saturday when he had come to drop her off. She said this, and her chest started thumping wildly. Saumya visits her on occasional Saturdays, hangs out for a little while, and leaves before it gets very dark. But that Saturday they came over from the university, and it got to be 9 o'clock before they knew it. Saumya could easily have gone then too, but then Saavali started feeling terribly scared, and she asked him to stay back, and her chest started its wild beat.

What about the dinner then? Saavali gets hers delivered home. Most times it is more than what she can consume. She eats some of it at night, and keeps the rest for breakfast next day. For today, she had already placed an order at around 8 o'clock for two meals. They sat for dinner at nine-thirty. Coffee after dinner.

They had had plenty of chats with each other. And from whatever the chats could reveal, Saavali had found Saumya to be the finest man she had met in her entire life. She couldn't hold herself back from going up to him whenever she saw him; it gave her an inexplicable thrill.

Can't say why she had this fear today. But she felt that Saumya should stay. Her fear seemed to subside as they drank their coffee. Saumya was saying something – how he loves going biking, how he can't get along with his people at home, what songs he loves, why he doesn't like old songs, how he likes poetry. When he said 'poetry' she remembered the poems she had located in that strange trunk in the dark inner room. She thought she should show him those poems, maybe that would settle her fear. So Saavali told Saumya, 'Arey, once, you know, I found some strange kinds of papers in a trunk in that inner room, some kind of poetry, y'know! Worried me quite a bit.'

Saumya laughed. 'What was in it?' he said.

'Wait, I'll show you.'

Saavali lit the yellow light of the inner room and brought

those yellowed papers out.

Saumya is sitting on the chair, feet resting on the bed. Looks so nice! Hair looks so soft! The air from the fan is playing with his hair. Saavali did not feel any fear.

Saavali handed over the papers and Saumya read through all three poems. 'Why should you have felt afraid?'

'It's not the first one, but the other two are so weird!' she said.

'How weird?' Saumya.

'What d'you mean how weird? I had begun to cry, really.'

Saumya laughed softly – 'saumya'.

Saumya's soft, 'saumya' laugh brought Saavali to laugh too, and she also felt like putting her arms round him.

'You might have felt frightened,' Saumya said, 'but these are lovely poems.'

'I didn't understand, baba,what this poetry said.'

'This is what poetry is.'

'Okay, forget it. Hey, what movie do we see today?' Saavali had tired of hearing about poetry.

'Whatever you say,' said Saumya.

'Okay, let's see this one then.'

After that they spent a little time talking about the movie and a little more time laughing. Saumya sat in the chair and Saavali sat on the bed. The laptop was on the cot as they saw the movie. Around sleeping time, Saavali felt the same strange joy again. What would Saumya be thinking? Should I give him a hug? What could he have found in the poems? If he is so fond of things like poetry and stuff, how am I going to manage? But then he had never talked about his love for poetry until today, so, maybe, it won't be such a hassle, after all. Good, good man, Saumya.

Saumya spread a mat on the floor to sleep, and she slept on her bed as usual.

Before going off to sleep, Saumya asked, 'Should I go and sleep on that cot inside the bedroom?'

Saavali laughed and said, 'Rubbish! Just sleep here.' Saumya laughed too.

Isn't he wonderful? Saavali felt very light and drifted off. Switched off the light and slept. She had decided to fall asleep looking at Saumya. Stay awake for a little while, so she could watch him go to sleep. But it happened quite differently. She just lay on the bed and drifted off to sleep.

She got up with a start at seven in the morning, without a memory of what had happened in the interim. Arey, how could I have fallen asleep just like that? She had wound herself tight in the sheet. Sad she couldn't see Saumya drift into sleep. Well, she could see him now. His covering had gone awry. He was sleeping on his right side, with his back turned towards her.

Look at the way he's sleeping! Should at least have been facing this way! The covering awry and the T-shirt drifted up. He looks so fair! She had the urge to push his T-shirt up and see the colour of his back. The thought made her laugh at herself. She pulls up his shirt, and then she pulls it right off, and she sees his fair body. Oh, what mad thoughts! She threw away her covering, gathered her hair up and secured it with a clip that lay on the table. She went towards the basin to brush her teeth. She turned around and she could now see Saumya's face. His mouth was wide open and he was drooling on the pillow. She first found it weird. How could he be sleeping like an infant? For a moment she thought of waking him up and telling him about the drool, and to keep his mouth closed, couldn't he? But then she went on towards the basin for her brush and paste. She pressed some paste out on the brush and looked up at the mirror. She saw her own complexion. She does look nice, oh yes, but she's so much darker than Saumya! He has such lovely lips and mine are so dark!

She peeped out into the hall while brushing. Saumya's posture hadn't changed, but his mouth was now closed. Then, as always, she drifted towards her regular spot by the door.

Light there was aplenty, but the sunrays hadn't got in as they do. It was coolish, the light. As always, she folded her left hand behind her back and brushed her teeth. The wind was cool too. She gave her face a good scrub. Used soap to wash her face so early in the morning. She was doing all this for Saumya, of course, but she just thought she should soap her face. Face washed, she went into the kitchen to boil the milk. Put the milk on sim for boiling, and stepped out to the grill door, and stood watching the outside world.

Saavali felt great today. The sunrays had begun to steal in. The wind was quite cold. She could feel the wind on her legs through the shalwaar, and she felt nice. Some very old memories came drifting in. When she was in Pune University, it had such a lovely campus! She did a lot of loafing around there. It's a lovely ambience here too. How I've grown! Should she speak to Saumya about marriage? Far away she espied a flock of birds flying. Should go out for a walk. When is this guy going to get up?

Saavali stood looking out. She'd fallen into a reverie, actually. It was really so quiet out there, she just gazed and gazed. Just then she felt Saumya's arms come from behind her and wrap themselves round her. For a brief moment she didn't quite register. When she did, she loved it. How could Saumya have suddenly turned so bold? But good that he had. He stood behind her with his arms around her. She felt her hair grazing his throat. She went on gazing outwards. 'Is it okay?' When he asked her this, she felt so elated that she turned around in his arms and hugged him. She could feel the warmth of the sun on her feet. She could feel his body pressed tight against her breasts. Knees touched too. Saavali realized then that he was the best among the men who had come into her life. Saumya wanted to loosen the embrace and step back, but she held him tight, and her eyes welled up with tears. She could think of nothing, nothing. She again turned around to face outwards, held his arms close to her chest, and stood gazing outside. Saumya held her from behind and stood leaning against the wall. She could feel the touch of every part of his body. She had, of course, forgotten all about the milk simmering in the kitchen. The wind was carrying away with it so many memories of her past days.

Third Context

One

The 'I' of the first context, that's who I am.

I.

I am an author. The person referred to in the first context is I, the author. And the person whose name shows on the cover is a thief.

Really. I mean, the guy with this fifteen-letter two-word name is a bloody thief.

How? I'll tell you.

I write. About two years ago, in 2010, I had written a novella called *The Story of Being Useless*. Now this bastard got it printed under his name. You may well be finding all this a bit strange; what's all this that I am saying? And as you read this book, you think it has been written by the person whose name appears on the cover. But that's not how it actually is.

It's I who am the author of this book, and it's I who am the author of the novella that was published as *The Story of Being Useless*.

But now it's his name that shows on the cover, and not mine. There are reasons for it. For one, I do think of myself as a hugely useless person (that was the context in which I had written the first novel). A second reason is that I never ever feel like I am finished with whatever I want to write, and so I don't consider it as ready for publication. I am forever involved in it. Forever and ever and ever.

This forever and ever and ever shapes itself out into a triangle. And I lie in some damned corner of this triangle. That's to say, the tangle that exists in that corner, I lie knotted up in it. How many possibilities exist of triangles entangling with each other, I don't know. Each triangle carries its own context. When the context is carried from one corner to the next, words get scattered along the line. Walk along the line of those words, and it gets scream-time; topple outside the triangle, and it's emptiness; topple inside, and that's entrapment. Words that carry the context of meaning, and the triangles that form with words as lines. So, whatever triangle of story I am in at any given time, I just get trapped in one of its corners.

That makes my scalp explode. But I stay involved, and never feel that my work has reached completion. And that's exactly why I would never, never till kingdom come, get sucked into the business of getting it published (or that's how I think right now). But this thief is a little smarter in these matters. Whatever he wants to pilfer, whatever I have written, he just copies it out, and gets it published as a book.

That's the reason why I tell you, the person whose name is on the cover is a thief. The real writer is I. The chap on the cover is a fraud.

I cannot say, of course, that my behaviour is totally above board. The reason is this: that as I write, I know that it will be stolen and published. I am altogether aware that however incomplete I consider my writing to be, it is going to land in the hands of this person hungry for recognition, and it is going to be published. But that doesn't stop me from writing, does it? And that doesn't make me a particularly honest person, does it? But after all that, it can be said that I *am* an honest person. Even if nobody else says it, I certainly think I can call myself honest.

All this must truly be confusing you. Like, you would have bought this book, or borrowed it from a library, or somebody would have given it to you, or you would have found it somewhere, or some such thing. This book is of course an English translation, but the original Marathi one is not likely to appear as an ebook. This one may not either, so it is unlikely that you are reading it electronically. But if you are reading it some time after its first publication, well, then you may be reading an electronic version, or some other who-cares-a-damn version, or maybe a tattered page, or maybe just this single tattered line. But you would by now have got more and more confused.

What were those two earlier contexts, and now what is this guy blabbering?

I seek your forgiveness for all this. The person in whose name this book appears and I have been at loggerheads. For a long time now.

That fellow is very keen to earn himself a name.

Have I a yearning for a name too?

Unlikely, no.

My head is really reeling. Please can I change the topic a little?

All right, changing topic, please.

I seek your forgiveness for this too. But it feels like my head is really emptying out. It's become heavy from all sides. And it feels like it may explode, so I am changing the topic. Please bear with me. Apologies once again. I'll talk about this later. But as of now, I'm changing the subject.

Two

The guy of the first context in whose office I sat is my friend. He's my friend still. But we don't meet as often, because his office has shifted. The landlords have put the building up for sale. A new construction will come up there, so the old stone building is not going to stay there for long. Since it had to be put up for sale, all those office tenants were made to vacate. So, I can't go to that office now.

When I wrote about him, I was a frequent visitor at his office. I would go around lunch time, or post lunch, and hang around there till evening. That was when I had thought of writing about him.

First of all, that office was a lovely place, and it makes me feel sad that we've had to abandon it. The room that was used as an office was a sturdy old place. Therefore, however timid one was, it was still possible to sit there. Even if I am timid, the building and the room were such that they supported me. All told, then, it was a joy to go and sit there.

One could see the road from the left window. There was a gulmohar tree on the other side of the road. There was a doctor there in the building, directly visible from the window. Patients could be seen visiting him, and if some of these patients happened to be good-looking, one got to see them. The iron bars of the window were rusted, but they were good still. There was an umbar tree outside. All told, it was a grand place, that room. And therefore good. It was sad, then, having to move out. There was no remedy, though. The building did not belong to me, I wasn't a tenant there either, and the building, along with all the land that surrounded it, was worth crores of rupees. It was way beyond my means to buy. Going there, therefore, stopped, and I did what was within my means – write.

Secondly, I wrote because I believe that this friend is much stronger than I am. Not in physical strength, but if one were to examine the strength of living life, I believe he was stronger than me, so I wrote. The writing offered me great relief. There were a number of things about him with which I didn't agree, but I didn't bother about them. I mean, I gave more importance to the strength he displayed for living life.

Let me tell you a little more. I was doing my Master's in Political Science. I couldn't bring it to a satisfactory end, meaning, I didn't complete the course. I got bored towards the end, and just let it go. Loss of interest was one reason, and the other reason was that I had to think about earning money. Why did the need for money arise? Mmm, I don't think I need to take you into this private zone, and you shouldn't want to come either.

Well, then, so as to be able to earn a certain minimum

amount, I put my earlier typing certificate to use and got myself a job with a newspaper for typing out advertisements and notices. I am still with that job. Knowing both English and Marathi typing gave me an advantage. I go there from ten to two, and type out heaps of advertisements. I get six thousand rupees, and I need the money.

The typing course I had done was so unimportant, and so cheaply got that I don't even remember why I went for it. But it benefited me, all right. And, well, this work is quite good too. No stress in the head. Stress on the hands, eyes and back, yes. But I do it for the six thousand rupees. Not required to think at all in this job. It was only in the early days that I had some bother. For the first two or three months I would see letters everywhere dancing on the finger: a s d f g h i u p m. And then they began giving me Marathi ads too.

By and by I settled into the work.

But it's also true that my awareness of my timidity has grown sharper during this period. And because of that, when I went to his office, I became aware of his strength, true again. Oh yes, true all right.

So, yes, things were getting along quite nicely. And then, when it was decided to put that building up for sale, and I learnt that the office would fold, I felt sad, and took to writing about him. I know very well that I can't get into fabrication work like him, and I also know that I cannot do plenty of things the way he does them, so I put it all into a story. Touché.

This friend of mine did poetry, but –

– I don't care one little bit about discussions on poetry. Well, actually, as far as the issue of poetry is concerned, I can happily pick up a book of poetry that I like, and sit reading. That said, I can sit reading a book with, if possible, no poetry at all. But this kind of book doesn't exist anywhere, so why talk?

But when I move out for a cup of tea before leaving for office at 9 o'clock, I run into some poet, and the boredom begins. I don't understand what age I am living in. There are lots of people who write poetry. A little too many of them write poetry. No objection to people writing poetry, of course, but then they want to recite it, and that's when they start giving brain fever to others. Not content with that, they keep talking a lot of bilge in their effort to prove that they are poets. As an upshot, what I see around me is that the ones that talk are the ones who are poets. But hey, what's all this going on? I sit writing this in 2012, and I don't know which year you are reading this in. And here I sit, under these circumstances, calling poetry names! How's this going to help? There are, after all, good poems in the world! So then, what? Just sit reading our own poems to ourselves and stay mum? But as of now, there are just too many poets around. And poems too have mushroomed like crazy. When I notice any of this, well, I run. On the stage, on blogs, on Facebook, I see poems swarming all over these places and I run. When I run into a talkative poet, I run particularly hard. Like mad.

Let me change this subject right here, because there is nothing much to say about it, and there is no point in saying much about it. Writing stories is so much better.

Three

Before I begin writing stories, I feel annoyed. But –
– I really shouldn't get annoyed, but I do. I feel angry.

I'll tell you an incident. I was travelling by bus once. Not too many people in it. And this bus suddenly jolted to a halt. My head went and hit against the steel pipe of the front seat – bang!

It came out that somebody had deliberately brought his two-wheeler right in front of the bus. The driver was about to let loose a volley of abuses when the two-wheeler guy himself entered the bus from the front. 'Who spat that paan? Who's that son of a whore?' I almost began laughing, but held back. His greenish shirt was spattered all over with red paan spittle.

I was sitting on a right side seat, but I hadn't noticed anyone spitting out. Had to be somebody sitting behind. So this hulk of a man walked in. Six foot, at least, if an inch. But he hadn't done me any harm. 'Who spat, huh? Who spat? Who?' he growled, as he moved down the aisle. And then a skeletal scarecrow of a figure in a dirty white shirt and a dirty dhoti stepped out into the aisle with folded hands and sat right down in the middle. With folded hands he begged forgiveness of the hulk. Chyaayla! The hulk just didn't know what to do! Stumped! Finally, he just muttered 'Maadarchod,' and stepped out from the rear exit. He removed his two-wheeler and the bus started.

The old man was so awfully old that nobody could have done anything to him.

At first I felt quite amused. Then suddenly felt very angry. Angry at the entire bus. That's why I write. Does this happen because of the realization that there is no point in getting upset over people? Oh, well, forget it. I have to be reaching office.

It feels nice once I reach office. I-t space f-e-e-l-s space n-i-c-e space o-n-c-e space I space r-e-a-c-h space o-f-f-i-c-e stop. Once in a while I wonder why I am in this typing business. For the six thousand rupees, of course, that is the principal reason. There could be other jobs! But this doesn't cause mental hassles. Besides, I am free after two in the afternoon. I get time to visit his office. Got... no longer get... got, now, got time. What do I now do with all this free time?

I must look for another job. Will do so once I finish writing this stuff. The good thing about this job is that it gives me very little mental bother. The office people supply the pages. Details of the advertisements and notices just have to be keyed in. It's a newspaper office, so the hustle-bustle begins only late afternoon; there's nobody here before that. Just three-four persons pottering around here and there. I can also use the internet here for a good while. With all these advantages, this job looks good. But why should you be interested in all this, really? So this subject changed too.

Four

I do feel disgusted, I tell you. What happens really is that I get disgusted. Then I write, and the stuff that I write the chap whose name is on the cover pilfers and squanders.

I've stopped feeling anything about it now. Probably this is all that he does: pilfering what I write and getting it printed under his own name. Why should he be doing this?

But why the hell should I bother about why he does this?

I should just sit and write whatever I want to write.

But now, why do I write?

Why do I write? A girl had asked me this question. It's not as if I answered the question because it was a girl that asked. The girl was dusky, and the really amazing thing was that she was named Saavali too – dusky. So I responded to her. Dusky Saavali: everything about her fitted so neatly that I couldn't hold myself from responding. 'As a pastime,' I told her. The word 'pastime' amused her, and she laughed as she repeated, 'Pastime'. (I wanted to write a story about her. The 'Second

Context' from this novel is an attempt gone awry due to my inability to write a story about her. She was quite different from what I have written. I am telling this to you for no specific purpose. I won't say whether what I am telling here is true or false.)

I was just purposelessly wasting my time then doing a Master's in Political Science. Don't know why I was doing it. It's not as if the subject lands you a quick job. As far as I know, most of the guys let the main subject go and do something altogether different. So much better, then, that I let go of the Master's degree. At least I kept the study of political science going, and got to understand that everything is politics. Everything is politics. It's part of nature.

Talking, writing, walking – everything that exists is part of the politics. So, in a way my asking that girl about Ram Manohar Lohia and writing about it is my political statement indeed. But my pompous talk is not going to make any change in the overall political situation. That is also okay in a way. But, my writing here would surely be important for the politics of the overall existence, and more than that it is important for me at least. Otherwise, I now have no contact with that girl. That's why I have to come here in this library after I wind up the office work.

Five

I now come around 3 o'clock and sit in this library. Stay here till around seven in the evening. After the closure of my friend's office, I had needed a place for whiling away time, and this is a nice place for that purpose. Not many people visit this library. Basically, it's a small library. There are plenty of books here. It's nice and quiet.

I've got myself a nice corner. It's a survival need for me. There's a table and a chair in the corner. A window in front too. There's a beaten track outside the window, and there are some trees.

My head aches quite a lot, so I need to come and sit in this corner in the library. And I get time to write. I write. I have to write. All that I type is writing too.

Since my friend's office closed, I've snapped all contact with that place. My visits there have stopped, so to that extent my contact has snapped. But I didn't like that snapping, and felt like reconnecting. So then I wrote it all out. Sewed it all up like a patchwork quilt. Brought it all together, completely. And then I felt better. You know how one feels wrapping oneself in a quilt in winter and rolling up in a corner? That's just how I felt. Would I be able to express in words my thoughts about a quilt? How does one feel completely wrapped in a quilt? If it's a morning, one can see different colours of the patches on a bright background. At night, although the colours won't be visible, the different patch-sizes can be recognized and also the darkness falling from the small holes in the quilt. A quilt – strong and warm. That's how all the story was stitched up inside in my head and then I pushed it aside.

I wrote also because I had to establish a connection between the office and this library. Adding this little patch to the quilt makes it look nice too. And comfortably warm. I love these colours. Whatever there is in the ambience of the library is what I had found in the ambience of the office. What exactly it was, and is, I am still searching. Haven't found it yet. I search for it every day. And that is why I will never feel that this story is over. And that is why I'm going to be awfully angry when the guy whose name is on the cover pilfers this subject and gets it printed. But before I get into a rage and give myself a headache, let me change the subject.

Six

When I was doing my Master's in Political Science, we had this girl in class called Saavali. I finally abandoned the course, and I have no contact left with whatever goes on there. The girl was nice, but I couldn't really talk much with her. Just didn't have the opportunity. In fact, if the truth be told, I was quite timid, as I have mentioned earlier, so I couldn't create an opportunity. Well, never mind. I at least got to hear an unusual name. Wonder who would have named her. I've never heard this name before. Nice name it was.

I remembered her because what I can see inside the library and outside is shadows – 'saavali'. I so often keep disappearing into these shadows, these 'saavalis'. You are not going to believe it. You are not going to believe it, and that's exactly why I have to write the stuff out.

Oh, the shadows here are danger. When I got here, the sun was nice and bright, and the leaves of the peepal tree in front looked black from this side, and such a horde of their shadows fell here inside the library! It was a crowd of shadows inside here. Every single leaf had cast its shadow here. Besides, there were the shadows of the little stems that joined the leaves to the branches, and the branches themselves, each one. All these multitudes of shadows had left no place for me in the library. Beautiful to look at. Shadows spread across from end to end, and they rocked when the wind blew.

And then I got the sensation that these shadows were spreading out. I mean, it felt as if the entire library was getting taken over from the inside by these shadows. In fact, really, that was exactly how it had begun to happen. The shadows had subjugated everything in sight. It went on getting darker and darker, and I just vanished. I couldn't see my arms, my legs. Everything had been swallowed up by a black, black darkness.

What could it be? Where had I landed? For the life of me, I couldn't tell.

I had to get out of it. I swung my limbs wildly, tried to run this way and that, but it made no difference. I was startled a couple of times. Chyaayla, what if I banged into something in this frenzied running, and got knocked dead? And I didn't want to die. This I know for certain, that I don't want to die.

When this veritable black darkness descends, past, present and future, all tenses lose meaning and form. Am I dying? But, hey, I don't want to die. So I have to write.

When such darkness descends one doesn't want to eat anything. One may be ravaged by hunger, but the desire to eat disappears. I was quite a good eater earlier. But now in this pervading darkness, visibility zero, what does one eat or drink? This is danger. I don't want it this way, but it is, this darkness is. It is, even if it is not visible. And it's going to stay, so I'll have to write about that too. However it wrings the stomach, write I will have to. Whatever it is, it's aiyyaacha ghoda.

Getting bored, are you, with all this prattle of mine about darkness and stuff? You could be, too. But there's serious danger here. And the reason why I write about it is, of course, because I dwelt there. Besides, when someone gets stuck in that labyrinth, he should be helped, shouldn't he? Because it is difficult. If I have to save someone from dying, this is the very least I can do, right? If somebody out there is shivering from cold, I should be offering a quilt. It doesn't require one to be generous or courageous to offer a quilt. If that someone is hungry he should be given some food at least.

I am hungry. It's now four-thirty in the evening. Tea is all that I'll get, because the library is situated such that tea is all that I can get. And that too in the stall that is to the left as one leaves the library. I tell him on the mobile, and the tea arrives.

It's very dark. Past tense, present tense, future tense, these are the primary rules of grammar. But they get destroyed in this darkness. Because one doesn't know what tense is running here, chyaaycha, and my belly is on fire.

Hey, give me some tea.

Tea arrives. I escaped.

Escaped.

Survived.

I am. Am.

Not going to die. Will live.

I now have to come out of all this, so I write. And for getting you out of this too, I change the subject. Come along.

Seven

In Norway, a year ago, a guy blew a solid seventy-seven persons to death. Bombed eight and gunned down sixty-nine. A single man did this in a single day. What a fricking world!

One advantage I have of this library is that I can read a lot of magazines. This reading at least I do. Can't read too many books, mostly, but these magazines I read quite a lot. Whatever little I understand from them, I relate to. I know you are so much smarter than I am. I am just an ordinary typist, and I have not even been able to finish my Master's course in Political Science. But I'll tell you, anyway. I feel quite nice about these Scandinavian countries. I had wanted to visit them too. Relatively, they have a nice way of life. They get their Nordic models ready, spend on education and health, have a nice system running, is what I feel sitting in this library. Not many would want to disagree, anyway.

But in a place like this, if a guy blows up straight three-fourths of a hundred people out of disagreement on religion, what the devil should a person do then?

I've not talked on this subject anywhere. But it's given me a jolt, all right. There's no saying anything about anything at all. Just the other day the court there sentenced the killer to twenty-one years in jail.

But I have to confess my admiration for the defence counsel. He was a member of the Liberal Party, and he was given the responsibility of presenting the case for the killer of seventy-seven people. The lawyer's stance was that in a democracy, it's important to accept a responsibility of this kind. And so he agreed to defend the accused. Wonderful! And nobody went and beat him up or any such thing. He did his job, the judge did his job, and within a year the episode was brought to a close, at least to the extent of that particular episode. But, at root, seventy-seven people were killed. How come?

The world is a danger place.

Fact is, many more were killed here in Mumbai than in Norway. That's big danger too. But that happened when I was in the middle of writing my previous novel, and that kept me from flying off.

It's because of this Norway now that I've had to write.

Since this subject of guns has cropped up, let me tell you another story. It was a small town. I was quite small, and I was crossing a lane close to a shop named Sundar Kalaavastu Bhandaar. There's an excavation in the land for a gutter to pass through, and there's a ten-foot or so bridge across it. There's a government-approved country liquor shop right at the other side of the bridge. Well, I was going past this shop.

I was in school then, very likely in the seventh grade.

There's a perpetual haze of raw spirit around the bridge. As I was walking past one day, a person stepped out of the liquor shop, pulled out a small pistol, and put it against my stomach. Bloody shit! Came close to dying there, I. I felt a slice of iron pressed against my stomach. Honestly, for the first few moments I just didn't register what was happening. But then there was not a soul to be seen nearabouts, and I couldn't fathom why this guy had put his gun to my stomach.

I'd seen pistols before. On policemen's waists, with security guards at banks; besides, I had even handled those air guns. But this one, very likely, was the real stuff. (It was the real stuff. Got to know of it next day.) No denying at all that I was scared.

The man was punch drunk. That shop is made of termite-eaten wood. Wooden slats for sitting. And there is a red curtain turned black with filth. That was where the man emerged from and stood rocking with his gun to my stomach. I didn't stir. What if I stirred and the gun were to go off? I could feel the pressure of a small round iron piece against my stomach. (I felt it for many days afterwards.) The man then began laughing loudly, and just toppled over into a patch of slush next to the shop, all by himself. I didn't have to move a finger. He just lay stretched out, left arm extended and the right arm with the gun caught under his stomach.

The next day I had proposed to go that way, just to see how things had proceeded, but before I could do that a nearby paan shopowner I knew brought the news that there had been a murder around that area. There is a sugarcane juice shop on the other side, and the owner's brother is a goon. He had nothing to do with the murder. Don't know exactly who this man was that died. I went past that shop a number of times, later on, just to see if I could spot the guy who had stuck his gun into me. The murder was committed with a gun, the paan person told me. It occurred to me that the very gun that I had seen was likely involved in the murder. But I never saw that man again. That grimy, rotting shop still stands. A few people visit it too. But I never saw that man again.

From then on I could never be impressed with the toy-like guns that heroes use in movies. Of course, I told nobody about why I felt that way. But having experienced what it feels like when a real gun is pressed against your stomach, I could never settle for the stuff that the heroes used on screen.

Now that this subject of heroes has sprung up, let me tell you another story. I was walking along the road once. Very early in the morning, seven-thirty. There was no traffic at all. Had to buy half a litre of milk. I had bought the milk, and as I was crossing the street, a two-wheeler came speeding from the right. I stopped, I did. But after all that, as the two-wheeler whizzed past, the driver shouted, 'Your aaicha daana.' I shouted back, 'Hey, you maadarchod.' There were two on the bike. Did not stop. But I had really lost it. I ran in their direction, milk pouch in hand. Of course I couldn't run at the speed of their bike, but there's a college nearby, and they were bound to be somewhere around, so I ran in that direction. There they were, the two. I nicked open a corner of the milk bag with my teeth, and threw it at them. It hit the chap sitting on the bike on his right shoulder and burst open. Milk all over. 'Your ayyachi gaand,' screamed the guy, kick started the bike, the pillion jumped on, and they raced towards me. This suited me very well. I first ran back. I ran back into my lane. As they appeared, I picked up a brick from the heap next to the neighbouring cycle shop, and landed it on the head of the pillion. Picked up the same brick and smashed the headlight, and threw it at the chest of the driver. The bike lay on the road. The pillion rider had scooted away, and the bike guy was too stunned to speak. 'Maadarchod,' I said, and walked away. They were junior college boys, likely.

I really shouldn't have done that, but they were trying to play heroes too, bastards.

I of course banged up only those people I could afford to bang up.

But it's been going on like everything is affordable.

But, even so, I shouldn't have done what I did.

But, on the other hand, good that I did. The bastards, it would have straightened them up a bit.

Or maybe it wouldn't have, too.

That's exactly why I have to write, chyaayla.

But very likely I didn't do any such thing. Yes, I traded abuses with them, that's certain. But I didn't throw the milk pouch at them. I didn't throw a brick at anybody's head. I didn't throw it at anybody's chest. Good thing too. I had felt like doing it, true, when we were exchanging abuses. But it's good I didn't bang them. If they had attacked me, I don't know what kind of scuffle would have resulted. But I myself didn't go beyond that point, and that's good, at least as far as this episode is concerned. There wasn't any need, either. It wouldn't have been right of me to have drained my anger on them. So, good that I behaved.

This confusion will go on going up and up and up. I said

things to them, was that good or bad? Should I have said more? Is this a kind of timid intellectualizing? If they had come face-to-face, some kind of give and take could have occurred, but how can a man's speed ever match the speed of a bike? I don't sit philosophizing, and before the confusion increases any further, I change the subject.

Eight

Subjects can go on changing. Not much would have been said on the main subject. But I keep checking out whether I can extract something about the main subject out of all the other subjects. And this bastard pilfers my subjects and gets them printed as his own. Can't really do anything about it. But I can write, and why I write was the fundamental context of this subject. But I just can't say anything at all on this issue. At least as far as I am concerned, I just can't talk with any clarity on this issue. But this guy who steals away my subjects, what do I do of that? Why does he want all these drums and trumpets for himself? And why is it that I can't stand up to him? The answer to why I can't stand up to him is quite simple – I am a spunkless gone-case.

You do think that I consider myself useless, don't you? Okay, well, let's try to get a hang on who you are. Where you live, of course, I'll never know.

Speaking of language, I sat and wrote this stuff in Marathi, and then it got translated into English. You are obviously reading it in English, then, or to really stretch it to an extreme, reading it in some other language into which it got translated. Agreed, yes, I am stretching things a bit too, too far. But considering that it doesn't harm anybody, this stretching, so, well, let's stretch then. You are on this earth, for sure, sitting or lying down and reading. And you'd very likely be reading it alone. If you are a lot of people reading this together, please don't do it. Read it all by yourself, as far as possible. Well, so, you are reading this, the stuff that I have written. I don't know who you are, but I am communicating with you. Where are you sitting? In a corner? On a bed with a covering or so? Or are you under the tin sheet of the shed? The one behind the market? Are you reading this book off pieces of paper, or using some technology beyond ebooks? Wearing something? What kind? Worn out or top of the shelf? How do you find this book? Could you be reading this after I am dead and gone? I hold you in the greatest respect, as you would expect from the language in which I address you.

But, of course, it doesn't always happen the way we expect it to happen, does it? So, then, whoever you are, whatever you are, please be. Stay happy.

I had it in mind to write about the friend of mine who does fabrication work. I wrote that, I did, but I hadn't finished writing. You read it, nevertheless, because that hungry-for-name bastard has gone and got it published. I sometimes feel that I quite pointlessly keep calling him names. But what am I to do? I can't really come to terms with it. I sit and write something here, make an effort at putting something across; and before I can finish, this guy gets after getting it printed, and gets it printed too! What kind of behaviour is this? Maybe he feels that I may die before finishing saying whatever I have to say. I mean, whatever stuff I write, I never feel as if I have brought it to any conclusion, so maybe he must have come to his own conclusion too. But why does he do this?

Or, to be very honest, why do I do this?

Why he does what he does is quite clear – he loves to see his name printed on the covers of books. I don't count for anything with him. The moment he feels that the matter is good enough to be published, he gets busy. My problem is that I can't stand up against him. I just don't have that kind of strength. If somebody starts pushing me around too much, well, that can be resisted. But this pilferer of my work, this guy I just cannot resist. The only thing I know is how to write, and it seems to me as if this guy has held me prisoner somewhere just for this. In a way, I fear him. Saalaa, does not let me go free, the bastard. Or nearer the truth, I can't shake myself free of him. Doesn't let me live the way I want to, bhadva. This abuse fits him, really. Am I overdoing all this? Am I getting you confused again? I mean, are you beginning to wonder why I should be telling you all about the strife between him and me?

What happened was, y'know, that when that girl asked me why I wrote, since then this bloody question has gone and settled deep inside my head. In fact, this question has been there since the time I began writing. But now, sometimes it gets to be beyond endurance. It brings relief then to just write it all out. I mean, it was always in my head to write about why I write. But he doesn't let me finish this either. I write some stuff, and he materializes, and checks out all that I have written. Takes whatever I have written to his office and types it out, so a soft copy comes into being, which he saves in a pen-drive. He comes, examines the papers, takes a pen-drive, examines the stuff inside, and walks off with it all.

It all gets beyond my understanding. But I have started staying cool these days. I have come to accepting his existence.

Another thing must be clarified here. Lots of writers have written about their own writings and the writings of others. Besides, the scientific angle there has also been laid out clearly by some of these science people. All of this you are bound to get somewhere out there. But what had been bugging my head was, is there anything else beyond that? I mean, beyond the primary stuff that all these people have been talking about. Not spurious, watered-down stuff, but something substantial, solid. That's what I had wanted to dig out. And this, I have realized after plenty of slogging and sweating, is not as simple as it seems. In spite of this realization, however, I still sit here turning over this thing and that. But now, I'm sitting here examining things, see? And this chap will come along and carry it all away. Drives me crazy, the bastard. Or probably, it could well be that it's I that hassle him, so from time to time he carries away whatever I have written and gets it printed. Reduces his hassles with this exercise, maybe. Best left alone, poor chap. Just let him be. Why should I bug him? I have done all that I can. Sunday is coming, and I'll get myself a good big sleep, and that'll put things back into order.

Nine

Except for Sunday, I go to office every day. Sunday doesn't need any announcing. But it happened the other day that I once went to office on a Sunday, quite by mistake. Climbed up five flights of stairs only to see that the office is closed today, it's a Sunday. I felt thrilled. The office building in its entirety is quite big. The office itself is just one floor. There are some other offices in the rest of the place. Most of the corners have been painted red with paan spray. Some corners are very dark. I went round the entire building today. Some classes are held on a floor on top. There were no classes, but two couples were seated on the stairs there. Didn't want to disturb them, so I backtracked and came down the stairs at the other end. It's a round building, and that's how I felt as I came down.

Everything looked different down there. This is not how it is every day. It looks very different today.

The parking looked strange too today. It was all so empty. My boredom got some rest. A hefty man was fixing his juice-cart. An oily person was fixing his vada-cart. A strong-built woman was clearing the mess in the building.

The amount of dust in the parking lot! Horrendous dust and stones. The entire two-wheeler parking layered in dust. Vehicles nosing into each other. And in the spaces left unoccupied – pigeons. Cooing away. Grubbing for insects in the dust. Grey pigeons. The grey of the dust coating the grey of their feathers. Cuddly pigeons hopping everywhere. And the emaciated parking-lot man finishing off his tot of hooch. The stubble-chinned fellow drinks out of a plastic cup. No constraints of time. His belly is actually a cavity. Burps. Comes to this parking corner just for his tot. For the rest of the time, his job is to keep things in order.

> After some prior confabulations
> The flock of pigeons up in the sky
> The dust on their wings gets in the air
> Dust in the drunk's eyes

'Abey maadarchod!'

Drunk flings abuse to the dust.

All this was going along so peacefully that everything had gone calm. My head went really cool. Turned lighter and lighter. Felt like bringing everything to a stop. Everything to stay as it is, where it is. Juice-man, vada-man, cleaning-woman, parking, dust, drunk, pigeons, occasional gust of wind, the grime-laden building with all its this-and-that, gather all of it up and keep it permanently somewhere. Absolutely perfectly quiet in the head, silent, incomparable. Freeze. Freeze. Right here. Beautiful.

But it doesn't stop really. It can't be stopped. What is

beautiful to me may not be beautiful to the next person.

That was why I got started.

Got started, and there, at the edge of the crossing stood the short old man, poor soul, thick spectacles, white shirt worn out from behind, dark grey trousers, slippers with vanishing soles. Calendars in hand.

Another new year has arrived. Today? Chyaayla, and I didn't even know.

The old man's right arm, bent from the elbow and extended across and forward. And from the strong, stubby fingers hang the calendars – two of them. More calendars in the bag in the left hand. On the left wrist, face turned inwards, a watch, the winding kind. The seconds hand constantly in motion. For the rest of the year the old man sells cotton wicks. The entire sky gathered in his eyes. Humungous, big, stunted, small man. Where did he get such strength from? Hey, say something. What's going on in your head? Nothing that I can ever understand, is it? Well, okay.

The old old man. I am floored. In the presence of this phenomenon, I am floored.

The old man was here the previous year too. Another new year has arrived. Got closer and saw that the calendar read 2013.

The cost of one calendar was only twenty-four rupees. The old man is selling twelve months for two rupees each. The months and years have got cheaper, it seems. Has time itself gone cheaper nowadays?

The old man would never indulge in such crap. He would just laugh. Does he have thirty-two teeth or just twenty-four?

Can all this be brought to a halt right here for a little

while? It shouldn't be brought to a halt, of course, but can it be frozen just as it is? For a little while? The old man's eyes are loaded with the poignancy of years and years. And his unbounded strength!

What an invincible person stands in front of a sissy like me! What do I do?

Write?

All right.

– That is exactly why I had to lay out this entire mess.